VOLUME 1

CRAFT

ELEMENTAL GODS

THE PHANTOM WRITER

CONTENTS

CHAPTER ONE

The sky cracked right before Sykes' eyes. All he could do was to watch.

Vulcan was there, too, right next to him; an innocent two year old watching the world end whilst laid out on the grass in their back garden.

Sykes' first instinct was to reach for his son, yet he couldn't move. The crack in the sky widened as if some pair of invisible hands had clutched at the seams from the other side of it and pried it open some more.

No, Sykes groaned. *No no no. Vulcan.* He thought he was gritting his teeth, but his mouth couldn't move, either. *Come on, come here! Shit!*

His attempts were futile. He tried to turn his neck; nothing. His hands registered the itch to move, but yet again, nothing.

Come on! Move, you useless asshole! Move!

The tear then distorted, spinning wildly and forming into a swirl akin to water getting sucked down a drainpipe.

The air left Sykes' lungs and he was uncertain whether it was from the tear or out of panic.

His eyes were wide open, as if someone pried them and froze them just so he could witness it all coming to an end.

Vulcan wasn't crying.

Still, not all movement was gone. Sykes could feel something churning inside of him. It was a heavy, dark boulder, rolling itself bigger and bigger over his heart.

Dread? He thought, and as soon as he did, the label stuck. *But for what? There is nothing to dread about my life. 31 years—no career, no future, no love-life. Ah...that's it, she's gone too...Montana...I could dread that, I suppose.* As the boulder rolled all inside of him, the sky continued to crack, the black swirl expanding, as if swallowing the entire world. *Vulcan, too,* he continued, *watching him grow...I will lose all that. I will miss seeing him make something of his life, hopefully...*

Sykes wanted to turn and talk to his son, to let him know that his footsteps are not to be followed. Yet he was stuck watching the sky dissolve into darkness.

All of a sudden, a howl erupted out of the swallowing swirl. An odd shape flung itself right out. Sykes' paralysed eyes were enough to see that that shape was trying to keep itself afloat and failing.

A second passed, then another, then a third. A giant claw burst out through the swirl, sitting still a moment then turning like the head of a snake in search, and, upon finding nothing, it lashed itself at the sky, slashing through and blindingly reaching for the floating figure.

Upon contact, sparks surged in all directions, coming down like fireworks in reverse, yet ones which quickly fizzled out of existence without a *pop*.

The sparks were followed by blood. The *blood* did not fizzle. It rained down and splattered over Sykes' face. A droplet entered his right eye, tinging half the world in the same crimson hue.

It all happened in a flash from there. Another swirl appeared, yet this one seemed to move over the length of the claw, swallowing it whole, leaving no more trace of it.

With it gone, the odd shape in the sky floated along for a couple more seconds before its hurtling descent was made obvious.

It crash landed right into Sykes' yard.

LET ME MOVE! Sykes' howled within his head, *Vulcan, I swear. I swear I tried. My strong man...my...Vulcan...I swear Pops tried...I swear it to you I—*

The figure rolled into Sykes' field of vision. The face was obscured by the blood pooling in Sykes' right eye.

"You," the figure said. Its voice did not appear human, but rather coated in a robotic tone. "You—you *must* do."

What? Sykes hoped to be able to ask, yet he was still paralysed. *Do what?*

"I'm sorry," the voice continued. "I'm so sorry. There is no time. I wish there was. It's not your fault, whoever you are. It's really not. But it *cannot* die with me. I'm so sorry, you two."

You two?! No no! Leave Vulcan out of this. Come on, wait, what are you—

There were no more words after that. In their stead, a flash burst into Sykes' eyes—a flash much brighter than the sun itself. At first, it was nothing but light. After, that light was momentary peace that spread over Sykes' whole being.

You are all and nothing, strange words entered his mind. Words that had about them the air of belonging to some greater thing and not just a man. **You know everything and nothing. The world exists to be touched—to be grabbed and harnessed. The mind is a silent place, but yours will fill with noise. It is the voice of the world. The world is all and nothing. Speak and it will listen.**

And so Sykes listened. As he did, everything vanished.

Sykes woke up with a fright. He sat up and turned towards Vulcan, flinging a stack of papers off his chest.

The boy was asleep on his back, seemingly unperturbed. Sykes ran a soft finger over his chest just to make sure that he was breathing. For some odd reason, he felt the need to check for blood. He looked all over the baby's round head for any splotches and even ran some hands over his own head.

Nothing.

No matter how hard he tried, he couldn't tell himself why he was doing it.

He even looked around the yard for signs of *something*, unable to tell what that was. When he found nothing, disappointment bubbled up inside of him and he didn't know what to do with it and so he gave up, turning instead to the many papers spread out all around him.

His stomach turned upon reading the name *ICARUS* atop them all. The disappointment seemed to grow inside of him as he started picking them up, each glance he threw over the contents of the reports making the feeling harder and harder to deal with.

An innocent yawn pulls him back from his temporary despair. All the papers were back in a clump as he turned towards his son.

"You're awake, are you?" he chuckled, scooting closer to him. He put the papers down at his side and went to pick Vulcan up.

The baby started to giggle and squirm, his little hands looking for something to grab onto. "What is it with you?" Sykes asked him, "what do you want? I'm not your mother, I can't talk to you as well. You're two, right? Give me some words to work with."

But Vulcan just squirmed around some more. Sykes softened his grip and let him turn around in his hands until he could see that his son was reaching for the papers.

Sykes let him have a few.

"Good thing you can't read yet," he chuckled. "Otherwise you'd be just as let down as I am."

He watched his son bring the papers to his mouth. Part of him wanted to stop him, but then he saw that Vulcan was chewing down on the name *ICARUS* and decided to let him.

"You get them, boy," he said, "if I can't, then at least you."

Sykes sat himself down on the living room sofa, staring at the dark screen of his TV.

Vulcan's *coos* and *caas* from the other room were a soothing thing to the mind, not due to the nature of the sound, but because it meant the little rascal was well asleep and couldn't cause a ruckus for a little while.

He was quick to dispel all that had happened earlier as a bad dream. It wasn't his first experience with sleep paralysis, after all. He took a deep breath, and, as his body shifted, he grew aware of the papers in his lap.

Sykes' application to ICARUS.

7th time's the charm? He asked himself, a little smile on his face.

There was no point in looking through it. Nothing has changed about him since the first application. Same jobless man living in his mother's home. The flames beneath him were starting to bite at his ass, though. All the inheritance he's gotten was already running out.

Bound to, he thought, *2 whole years of existing just off your money, Ma, things are 'bout to run out.*

He took a deep breath, trying to calm himself down.

I don't want to sell the house. Where would Vulcan stay? With his mother, I suppose, but—no. I...I need to be in his life. I can't be like father.

He grew restless. His skin prickled up and started to itch all over. There was no point in what he was feeling. Nothing would change. Nothing *has* changed. Even so, he kept on to his foolish dreams.

That was the thing about a dreamer. His eyes are always turned towards the brightness of an imagined future, so much so that he tends to ignore the darkness of his surroundings. So detached, he is, that he could be up to his neck in it and not care.

To take his mind away—to be able to keep it latched onto that bright future—he searched the sofa for the remote and turned on the TV.

Host: *So what I am to understand is that the world is changing, Ms. Clothos?*

Ms. Clothos? Sykes wondered. *What even is that name?*

He looked up in the corner and saw the programme logo: a *W* and a *C* glued back to back, shortening the post's name: *World of Craft.*

Whenever he could, Sykes watched it, hoping to find some secret into opening up his own mind to the wonders of crafting.

Ms. Clothos: *The world is **always** changing, even if we do not take into consideration Crafting and what it has brought upon humanity. Climate change is a rising issue, now, even more so than ever. Seasons are changing and—*

Host: *Sure, but we are not here to talk about climate change, we are here to talk about Crafting.*

Ms. Clothos smiles faintly, yet Sykes could tell that her smile wasn't her own. It was something she put on to appear more likeable.

Ms. Clothos: *This right here is humanity's problem, you see. It doesn't realise that **everything** is connected. Climate change will deeply affect the state of Crafting. Us, crafters, draw our strength **from** nature. We draw it **from** the fabric of reality itself. The more unstable that becomes, the more unstable our powers. Ignorance towards this fact alone stems from ignorance towards how Crafting works.*

Host: *How **does** Crafting work, for those curious to know at home?*

Crafting is the awakening of the mind towards the world's truth, Sykes repeated the tried and true phrase in his mind at the same time as Ms. Clothos, *it is—* he continued, but stopped himself as soon as he realised that the woman on TV was no longer following the same script.

Ms. Clothos: *... but the problem with that statement is that it's—*

Host: *Misconstrued?*

Ms. Clothos: *Outright wrong.*

Host: *Are you sure, Ms. Clothos? What you are saying goes against everything we know about Crafters.*

Ms. Clothos: *Everything you know are neatly packaged lies and express-posted to your front-doorstep.*

Sykes placed the ICARUS application aside and leaned forward, his eyes focused on no one but Ms. Clothos alone. She was a dark-skinned woman of an ambiguous age. Her eyes seemed to shine like gold under candlelight and her thick and long, just-as-golden dreadlocks fell down over the chair she was sitting on, wrapping around her whole body like vines. She held one in between her fingers, slowly, carefully, rubbing it together, as if it was some sort of close companion.

Ms. Clothos: *Any crafter worth their name will tell you that it is not* **truth** *that they've come to encounter, but* **lies**. *It is their* **own** *lies at that, too. I want you to take a moment and think how a man is capable of walking on water, or how one is capable of no longer needing air to breathe, making his lungs lose purpose. Do you sincerely believe there's some* **truth** *hidden in this world that makes such a thing possible? No, there isn't. The world works a certain way and what we, as a species, have always done best is to stand tall against nature and pound our chests, defying it every chance we get.*

At this moment in time, the host, a mousy young woman, pressed her hand against her earpiece, looking a little concerned.

Host: *Ms. Clothos, I am terribly sorry but it seems something has come up and—*

Ms. Clothos: *Don't worry, I won't be long now.*

Ms. Clothos sat up from her chair, her long dreads brushing the floor as she stepped towards the camera. Like living vines, they reached for it and fixated it on her face, a man's terrified scream echoing somewhere behind the image.

Ms. Clothos: *If truth is what the people want, then listen here: The **only** truth that exists in this world is that lies are our strongest weapons. The search for truth is the biggest lie ever told to humanity. The first man to ever utter such an idea has set our species on an endless, meaningless quest which has limited our potential. We are where we are by blind luck, and we will get where we are fated to get out of our own ignorance. Our fates are sealed and my attempt here to change them is nothing but that, an attempt.*

She got closer and closer to the camera, whilst people filled the background. The host was carried away as men stood there, with odd books in their hands, chains dropping from their corners onto the floor, pulsating with light as their hands reached towards the woman.

They, too, were Crafters. They, too, were trying to harness a world of lies in order to sell truth.

Ms. Clothos: *Close your minds to the lie of truth. Open your minds to the truth of lies.*

The program cut.

Sykes was on the edge of the sofa, his hands clutching at the pillows. His eyes were wide and his mouth parted as he found himself on the verge of screaming.

Close your minds to the lie of truth.

Open your minds to the truth of lies

The words floated inside of his mind all day.

What's that even meant to mean?

He checked to see if Vulcan was still asleep. He sat by his cot and stared blankly into nothingness.

She can't be right...right? Every Crafter, every study...every agency. Everything works on this profound understanding that the world is hiding something from us. It is humanity that must find this truth...

His leg shook, as if pushing down on a foot pedal attached to his brain, making it pick up speed, sewing a whole lane for his thoughts to race down on, one after the other.

But then—

Wait, if—

So what if—

No it can't be I mean—

A bunch of them sped up too much and ended up hitting against some bannister and into one another, cutting their lives short. But there was one thought that gripped Sykes like a noose, tying tightly around the neck of his brain.

*Hold on…*he suddenly sat up, the world slowing down, the noose loosening, allowing him a moment to breathe as he looked around. He paced away from the cot without a general direction. He just needed to be on the move. *If the truth were really all that was needed to unlock such capabilities, then, the moment one Crafter discovered it, then surely, if explained, it should be understood by others and replicated with ease. No,* he shook his head, *it can't be that simple…I mean. If **truth** is all it takes, then it should work like that…*

He suddenly hurried around in search of his phone. With it in his hand, he Googled some research papers on Crafting, especially the discovery of a Crafter's ability to thread on water with his bare feet.

Come on, his foot tapped, his teeth biting at his lips, *I've read this before, I remember. I just need to see the wording. I understood it then, but I didn't try. If I understand, then surely, I should **know** how, right?*

He quickly found it. His eyes scanned the words.

The secret, Lord Immanuel's—a Crafter belonging to some obscure royal house in Europe—retelling stated, *is realising that the world is built out of invisible layers, all stacked on top of one another. These layers are physical things, these layers can be touched. Even where there is air, a foot can press itself upon it and climb, a hand can grab and pull, a head can hit against if not careful. The layers are there, you just have to see them. It is not water that I walk on, but* **anything** *and* **everything**.

His eyes scanned and scanned, scrolling over the pages, latching onto anything relevant, trying to find the part he was thinking off. He scrolled down the whole PDF, skimming, pacing around the house until he found himself standing by his tub. Still scrolling, he ran the water, corking the drain and waiting for it to collect.

He didn't need it filled up. He just needed it to be filled enough so it was obvious whether his feet were touching the bottom of the tub or if he was standing on water.

Why water is mentioned, he continued reading, *is because I practised with it. I thought it easier to envision this invisible layer spreading over something* **visible** *and with more* **physicality** *than air. After doing this, I managed to walk on air and walk everywhere, and with that I...*

The level was good enough. He turned off the tap and stared at the water for a moment before returning to his phone.

All I did was keep my eyes closed and draw these layers over the world before me. I etched them so deeply that I could see their outlines even as I opened my eyes. That's all. That's all I did and...

After that, the paper rips away from Lord Immanuel's retelling of the events and gets into some complicated academic jargon that has always slipped right past Sykes.

He had what he needed. He set his phone aside, took off his dark jacket, cuffed his black jeans half-way up his shins and took a deep breath as he stepped into the tub.

The water was lukewarm and it settled around his ankles.

Alright, he closed his eyes. *See the lines, Sykes. It's simple. You see them, they are there, then you walk.*

Even then, as he was doing it, it didn't cross his mind that if that was the *truth* then he should have been able to simply do it the moment he knew that they were there. There didn't need to be no imagination, no etching, no drawing, no nothing.

But who could fault a man like Sykes—a man so desperate to do something *good* with his life that he believed anything and everything that was said about Crafters in the hopes that he, too, might become one?

Surely not himself.

It wasn't long before he saw the lines in the darkness. They traced the tub, they stacked in the air and over the water.

With his eyes closed, he lifted his right leg, just enough so the sole touched the surface of the water.

The line is there, Sykes. It's the truth! The truth, I tell you!

As he stepped down, his foot went right through and submerged itself.

"Dammit!" he hissed. "Again!"

Once more he closed his eyes, imagining the lines. Once more he stepped, once more it went through.

Again and *splash up* and

again and *splash down* and

again and *splash all around* and

again and *splash everywhere* and

again until he was all wet.

"It can't be," he sat by the edge of the tub. "Then...she's right?"

His whole body seemed to deflate. He looked over the surface of the water and upon seeing his reflection, for the first time in his life, he wasn't entirely certain of who was staring back, from where, and into what.

He had spent that entire day scrolling the internet whilst simultaneously watching TV, trying to see what the people were saying about Ms. Clothos' statement.

The TV programmes covered it vaguely, no one daring to say too much. Even some Crafters—all independent, for it was later found out that none of the present Crafting Agencies allowed their Crafters to speak on this topic—muttered more to themselves than into the microphones.

The online forums were where the chaos was at, Sykes quickly found out. Conspiracy theorists piling on top of one another.

>makes sense, doesn't it? why would these crafters want more like them?

>yeah, lmao. they can literally do all that they want. the fewer crafters there are, the

stronger those that already exist are.

>this is just a fucking hoax. you're all a bunch of lazy asses not wanting to bother

with doing the hard work of becoming a crafter. rot on your sofas fatsos

>are we just going to ignore the fact that they cut her out? Who does that if she's just spouting horsecrap?

>why would they let her spread propaganda?

> oh no! how dare they spread propaganda against my propaganda! the world is a

lie!

CHAPTER TWO

In the back of the cab, the following day.

Sykes was headed for Icarus HQ. His head was pressed against the window, his application at his side, Vulcan sleeping against his chest.

He stared out into the world. The odd splashes of the suburban yellow-green nature disappeared with each mile driven towards Chives Dale. Tall, gray buildings rose in unison and choked out the distant sight of Humphreys Peak.

That was man right there. If he's unable to build anything as grandiose as nature, he makes sure to make it ugly, barren, devoid of life, and he makes damn sure to make loads of it, to make it big and tall and to pack it real close and tight so any other sight is blocked out.

It's hard for man to build a mountain like Humphreys Peak, to put it shortly, but it sure seemed easy to make it go away.

Was it always like this? Sykes wondered.

He didn't get to do much wondering, either, which turned things more drab as the cab driver turned up the radio.

Well, folks, it appears that the prominent Crafter Agency Zalmoxis has ceased activity over night.

"What?" Sykes sat up in his chair, hanging by the driver's back rest.

"Some crazy shit out there lately, eh?" the driver looked in the rearview mirror, checking out Sykes' wide eyes. "'Scuse the language. You work for them or something?"

"No, no—I just—"

The press has not received a statement as of yet from Mr. Zalmoxis himself as to this sudden cessation. There is plenty of speculation travelling about, having grown its own feet out of nothing but odd statements from some Zalmoxis HQ associated Crafters in the wake of Ms. Clothos' statement.

It's caused quite a stir, hasn't it, Stephen? That statement.

Sure has. It gets ya wonderin' what's real and what's not, don't it?

"It does buck-all," the driver spat, turning down the radio. "Them Crafters are sinners, the lot of them. It's good that someone up there," he pointed his finger upwards, "is finally putting down the hammer. That's what you get, playing God and all.

So say," he looked back in the rearview mirror, "you one of 'em, mister? A Crafter?"

"Me? No." Sykes shook his head.

"So why we going Icarus? You lying to me, bub? I don't like being lied to. If you a Crafter you gotta tell me, it's in the constitution."

"Is it?" Sykes was absent minded.

Zalmoxis ceased operations...overnight...what...what does it mean?

"It damn sure is and so tell me before I cause a scene. Don't make a man cause a scene, you hear me? Not with a baby in the car."

"I'm not a Crafter," Sykes said, checking to see if Vulcan was asleep even with all the commotion.

"Then why we going there? What's that on your lap?"

"My application," Sykes sighed.

"You wanna be one of them?" the car came to a stop at a red light. The driver turned around and looked directly at him. "You not happy being a regular old folk, eh? With a wife and a kid, eh? That not good for ya? You wanna shoot beams out your ass, do ya?"

"I'm *not* a Crafter," Sykes croaked.

"Are you not? Then what you applying for? Janitor?"

"Yeah," he nodded, "janitor."

"Well I'll be damned," the driver cackled, turning around as the light turned green. The engine revved, Sykes was pushed back into his seat, his eyes distant, hazy, his mind just as so. "They need janitors, these Crafters? They ain't got no spark they shoot out their fingers to clean up the floor?"

"Beats me."

"Sure does. You're just a God-fearing man, is that what you're saying? You ain't no sinner? Sure as hell you'd love to be one, won't ya? I'll tell you what, I would, I mean—what man don't like a bit of sin, but some things, some things are too far they…"

The man raved on as Sykes sank further back into his head.

There was a lack of certainty within him, moreso now than ever. The hundreds of thousands of voices of strangers on the internet rang out in his head, so much so that he could no longer tell which—if any—belonged to himself.

He believed many things at once. All of them converged, closing in like hard stone walls seeking to crush him, squeezing the thoughts out of him.

He was incapable of holding onto them. As they appeared in his blank mind, they floated idly and then shot out, leaving nothing behind.

Sykes was just as blank as the cab came to a stop by the curb.

"Hey—hey, janitor, wake up," he whistled, "the Gods are waiting for you to mop their floors."

"Right, yeah," Sykes cleared his throat, sitting up awkwardly as he searched his pockets for cash. "Here," he dropped it in the man's palm. "Thanks."

"You take care out there. Don't be comin' outta there leakin' fire out your ears, y'hear?"

"I'll try," he slammed the door shut, "oh, wait," and then pulled it back before the man could leave, "I gotta take the pram out the back."

"Sure, yeah."

The driver popped the trunk. Sykes took the pram out, slammed the trunk shut, and, just as he got to unfolding it, the driver took off.

"You awake, big man?" he whispered to his baby, but his soft, hot breaths said otherwise.

Sykes carefully took him out of the carrier and placed him in the pram, pulling the top over so the light didn't shine in his eyes. He then unstrapped the carrier and placed it in the pram-storage area.

The whole time, Icarus loomed over him. It was the 7th time now that he stood in front of the building. Originally, it stood tall like a slick beacon of hope, its walls a circular, pure white, as if it was some tower trying to reach the heights of heaven. Yet the more often he stood there, looking up at it, the more it appeared to lean away, losing its footing.

"What the hell?" he thought, shaking himself.

Sykes pushed the pram inside.

"Mr. St. Jane," the Checker called his name. "Will you please pay attention?"

Sykes was mindlessly rocking the pram in order to keep Vulcan asleep.

"There's no need, is there?" he asked. He was sitting sideways on the chair; he hadn't bothered to turn. "I've been here plenty, haven't I?"

"It's protocol, sir," she pushed up her round glasses.

"Protocol or not, stop calling me sir," he finally turned his head, "please," he made sure to add. "Sykes is fine."

Clara flashed him one of her typical smiles. He didn't know for certain whether it was typical to her in general or just typical for her to flash it to him in particular.

Typical in some way or another for sure, though.

"Not bothered with a suit this time around either, sir?"

Sykes shook his head slowly. "Not my style."

"It's not about style, Mr. St. Jane, it's about proto—"

"I know," he said, "but is a suit really going to be what gets me in here?"

Clara smiled once more. "You never know."

"Didn't work till now."

"Sure," she scoffed, "but it's part of Icarus' requirements."

That is when Sykes raised his finger as if to stop her. "It's under *suggestions*, is it not? That's what I thought, at least."

"It is, yes," she confirmed, "but let's be clear, here, Mr. St. Jane, these sorts of *suggestions* are more often than not *requirements*."

"Well then make sure to write them under requirements. What's the point of that?"

"We're looking to see who is willing to go above and beyond for us," she smiled—again.

That smile irked him greatly.

It can't be her natural smile. It has to be something she is made to put on.

"Putting on a suit is going above and beyond?"

"It's much better than your casual fit," she shrugged, pursing her lips, "or bringing your toddler in with you for a Check."

"I'd say that coming in even when I couldn't drop my child off is proof of my dedication, not proof against it."

Sykes tried to smile. Clara did not return it. Her eyes instead wandered into the cot, watching Vulcan.

"Can I just put my hands in the scanner?" he asked.

"I'm not done reviewing your application," she sighed, leaning forward and catching her forehead in her hand.

"There's nothing new to find there, I mean—"

"I'm *not* done, Mr. St. Jane."

Sykes nodded. It was merely a formality by that point. Everything was the same each time he came. No other doors opened for him. No people came to meet him. It was only Clara that he laid eyes on and only Clara that he spoke with.

As his eyes rested upon his son once more, he pulled the pram closer, reaching his hand inside, grabbing his sleeping little hand and giving it a squeeze.

What will it take? He wondered, *things can't stay the same, can they? I don't want them to, I want things to—*

"I want things to change," he said it out loud instead.

"Pardon?" she looked up.

"I've been living a simple life for 31 years. I want that to change. I want to make an impact."

"We've had this conversation before," she waved her hand dismissively.

"I know, but each time, I meant it."

Clara sighed, setting down the papers as she propped herself on her elbows. She laced her fingers and rested her chin on the bridge they formed.

"Mr. St. Jane," she started, "this is your 7th—futile—application to us. I don't even want to know how many times you've applied to the other agencies and—"

"Only once," he said. "Only you allow denied applicants to apply again. The others don't."

"Right," she nodded, "either way. 7 times, Mr. St. Jane. Denied 6, and we're staring down the barrel of a 7th. I don't want to be rude to you, but how exactly is any of this change?"

"It's in your hands," he told her. "You can just say yes."

"It doesn't work like that."

"It could," he shrugged.

"Listen to me," she sighed. "Firefighters make an impact. Binmen, teachers," she smiled, "care-takers. Why not those?"

Sykes' eyes anchored to a point in space that was past Clara's shoulder. His mind wandered towards it and he quickly found himself traversing back in time, speeding right down memory lane.

—

The hospital machinery beeped. On one side of the man's bed sat Sykes. On the other, his brother, Lucas.

The two of them were holding the dying man's hands.

He was laid down, his face as white as the sheets that covered him. Tubes wrapped around his bed and pierced into his veins in hopes of spilling some vigor into him.

Sykes didn't know what was worse, that the man was dying, or that he had been dying like *that* for years.

What sort of life is that? He wondered.

It wasn't life at all.

"My boys," a weak voice trickled into the room. Sykes looked up, his eyes wide as they fell over the man's face. "You're both here."

"Of course," Sykes pulled his chair closer, squeezing the hand now with both of his. "Where else?"

"Your mother," his voice was like a sigh. "Is she here, too?"

Sykes and Lucas looked at one another. Lucas' eyes were rheumy as he said *yes*.

"Really? I can't see her."

"She's here, Pop."

The dying man smiled.

"You—we should call someone," Sykes looked over his shoulder, "tell them you're awake."

"No. Just the four of us."

"Right," Sykes nodded.

They watched him closely. Their eyes brushed over his face, years now since they've last seen it pulled by the strings of life, hungrily trying to take it in, hoping to immortalise the sight.

"There's something I've got to tell you," the man squeezed his fragile hands around his sons', "the *two* of you. Don't worry, your mother knows all about it."

"Tell us," the brothers said in unison.

"It's no secret. It's just a stone I've got to lift off my heart. I didn't have it in me to until now, my boys, I didn't."

"It's good, Pop," Sykes smiled, "it's good whenever."

"Your lives," he told them, "you do whatever you want with them. Don't let anyone, and I mean *anyone*, tell you what foot to place where."

"R-right."

"Look at me," his eyes dragged between the two of them, trying to see them both at once, but they were too far, oh, so so far, and each second he was pulled further, "your last memory of me, a shrivelled husk. I don't want you to remember me like this."

"We won't, Pop," Lucas squeezed tighter. "We sure as hell won't, goddamit."

"You will, you can't help it."

"We wo—"

"It's okay," he smiled. "It's not something you can change. It's how it goes. My father, too, I remember the last time we met. He turned his back to me and left for the woods, did I ever tell you that? He never came back. All I see now thinking of him is his hunched, dirty back. Of me, you'll see...tubes, a pale face, wet eyes. A pitiful man. Agh—" he winced.

"Pops!" Sykes stood, squeezing harder at his hand.

"Ahh...Jules," he smiled, "I feel you now. Were you there behind me all this time?"

Sykes and Lucas looked at one another. Behind their father was nothing but wall and cables.

"How...how I wish...to have gone out with a *bang*. I wish to have left you with something worth remembering."

"Pop, stop," Sykes' eyes finally filled with tears, "stop such nonsense. *You* are worth remembering. You don't need to do anything anymore."

"Ah..."

"You did enough. You took us in, you loved mother, you—you filled in our empty hearts. You...you did enough!"

"Did—did I?" he turned to Sykes.

"Yes."

"Well," he groaned, "I don't think so."

The slow pulsating beep of machinery suddenly cut, replaced instead by a constant, lifeless line. Sykes fell back in his seat, numb, as Lucas pressed his head against their father's chest, sobbing.

Chester St. Jane, a nurse's voice muttered somewhere distant. *Time of death...*

—

"Because I want to go out with a *bang*," Sykes said, "when the time comes."

Clara's eyes searched the man before her for *something* that he didn't much care for. She then nodded and returned to the application.

After a time of silence.

"And your child?"

"What about my child?" he asked.

"He will be happy for you to risk your life?"

"He should be as happy about that as he is about his mother and I forcing him into the world."

"That's..." Clara stopped, "sure."

"I *love* my child," he assured her. "I do this for him just as much as I am doing it for myself. I need to be strong, to have connections. The world is a dangerous place for non-Crafters."

"If you'll excuse me, Mr. St. Jane, but you didn't even have an epiphany yet. You're *not* a Crafter."

"I was bummed out about that for a while," he nodded, "until yesterday afternoon, to be precise."

Clara narrowed her eyes at him.

"I'm starting to think that what Ms. Clothos said was true. You're all a bunch of liars. Aren't you?"

"Mr. St. Jane..." Clara shifted in her seat, taking a deep breath, "let's...not discuss this right now."

"Sure," he smiled, "there's no need. I got my answer already."

With a sigh, she pushed his application even further aside, the sides of her eyes no longer peering at it.

"Everything is the same as before," she said blankly.

"I told you," he nodded.

"Your hands in the scanner, please, Mr. St. Jane."

Sykes let go of the pram and brought his hands forward. There were two rectangular holes on his side of the desk in which he placed his palms, turning them upwards. The machinery inside whirred as it started firing electrical pulses in his hands, shooting them up his body towards his brain.

It is said that a Crafter's brain is distinctly different from that of a normal human being. Upon attaining an epiphany—that is, upon realising *one* of the world's truths—a region of the brain that typically lays dormant and deemed useless, activates. With its activation, abilities are unlocked.

The scanner stimulates this particular region, sending pulses into it in order for *it* to send pulses back. Based on the speed and strength of these return-pulses, a Crafter's strength is determined.

"I've come off as a little hostile," Sykes said as he curled his toes. The electric pulses were no joke. "I didn't mean to. I *want* to be a Crafter, even if it means being a liar."

Clara looked up at him briefly, saying nothing.

"I'm sorry," he added.

"There's no need to worry. It's...volatile out there right now."

"We will retrieve your brain's response now," she said, hovering her hand over a small, blue button on her side of the desk. "Are you ready?"

"As ready as ever," he smiled.

The scanner got its response so quickly that it almost seemed as if the current got sent back before Clara even pressed the button.

Sparks surged out of the right-side hole, filling Sykes' hand with a melting heat that made him draw back his hand with a yelp.

"Mr. St. Jane," Clara jumped to her feet, coming around. She grabbed the pram, looked inside to see the baby was unharmed, and then gently pushed it aside. "Are you hurt, Mr. St. Jane?"

He simply shook his head. "I didn't feel a thing. Is everything alright?"

"I..." she looked down, perplexed, "I don't know. This never happened before. I...hold on."

She took a look at the scanner. Its blue, humming light flickered on and off as sparks continued to fly out. As she returned to her seat, Vulcan woke up, startled by the sound, and started to cry.

"Oh, come on, big man, you can't cry in front of Clara, she's *my* checker, it's gonna look bad!" Sykes smiled, picking up his baby, holding him pressed to his chest as he started cradling him, caressing his back. "Easy now."

Clara smiled for a moment as she picked up the phone receiver, buttoning a number quickly, yet as she held it to her ear, she realised the line was dead.

"Huh," she stood up, just *then* noticing that the lights in the room had all turned off. She made it for the switch, flipped it once, twice, three times; nothing. "Seem's we're out."

"Power outage?"

"Right as you were meant to be scanned," she sighed, pacing back, "look, I'm sorry, Mr. St. Jane, but we're more than likely going to have to postpone your Check. Could you perhaps come back another day?"

"Sure," he nodded, the baby finally asleep. He placed him back in the pram. "When?"

"I can't say for certain, but I'll call you."

"Personally?"

"*We'll* call you," she corrected herself, going to sit back down. "That's all for now. Thanks for coming and, well, sorry for...all this."

"No worries. Life can be a little unexpected, can't it?" he joked, "ever since yesterday the whole world's seems to be spinning the other way around."

"Yeah," she nodded, "tell me about it."

"Well," he unlocked the pram and spun it for the door, "see you when I see you."

"Good bye, Mr. St. Jane."

CHAPTER THREE

The taxi pulled up into the driveway. Her car was waiting there for him and she came out just as he was taking the pram out of the trunk.

"Thanks," he called to the driver as he took off. "Hey, Montana" he smiled at her, "how's things?"

"Good," she nodded. "Where were you? I've been waiting here ages." Her arms were crossed tightly. She looked from side to side, as if not wanting to be seen.

"Have you? I didn't notice I was running so late, my bad."

"You went to Icarus again, didn't you?" she leaned forward, furrowing her brow.

Sykes was in the middle of unfolding the pram as he stopped.

"You can tell?" he smiled awkwardly.

"It's all over your face, Sykes," she groaned. "You brought Vulcan with you?"

"Yeah."

"What did I say abo—"

"Come on," he rolled his eyes, "nothing bad happened. He was quiet, too. I rocked him the whole time."

"It's not *that*," she hissed, taking a moment to build her words, "it's just...those people...I don't want them around our son."

"Montana..."

"Don't apologise on their behalf, please," she shook her head. "Give him here," she reached for Vulcan, taking him out of the strap.

Sykes calmly handed him over. His fingers twitched from a burning pulse within his chest, spreading all throughout.

"What are you so afraid of?" his voice trailed with uncertainty. "That I'll become a different person?"

Montana stopped, pressing Vulcan against her shoulder.

"*Become*?" she asked. "Sykes...you've been a different person your whole life."

"Ah, come on," he rolled his eyes, "this again?"

"Until you get it through your head," she sighed. "It's pathetic, Sykes. You're like me—like us; normal people!"

"I should be whatever I want to be, not what you tell me I am, Montana," he stood his ground."

"Aha," she tightened her grip around Vulcan, "so you're a liar, then? Is that it?"

"Liar?" his face tightened, "where did you—was it the TV? Say it wasn't and I won't believe you."

"I've *always* told you them Crafters are a load of bull, don't pretend I didn't. I never understood it, Sykes," she shook her head. "You've told me so many times, but I never could wrap my mind around *why* you're so set on this."

Sykes was not much of a physical runner, but whenever met with Montana's harsh words, a twitch always sprung up in his hamstrings, ready to take him away. He never acted on it, although, damn it if he was ever as tempted as he was in that moment.

Instead, he turned his head up and glanced at the sky. A V-line of black, strange birds pushed beneath the clouds, their wings flapping in unison, their heads pointed in the same direction. Yet at the end of that V a straggler was beating unnaturally, trying to keep up with the rest. Sykes watched him fall behind, frantically trying to catch up, managing to keep pace for a little while before the struggle began again.

Not long after, the bird had changed its mind. It slowed down its flaps, narrowing its wingspan as it pulled away from the group, flying its own way, at its own pace.

"*Bang,*" Sykes smiled.

"Sorry?"

"Nothing," he shook his head. "I was in my own head."

"That's *exactly* the problem. You're in there too much. Out here," she waved a hand around, "way too little. It's not good, Sykes."

Sykes shrugged. "I might get in, you know," he said to her.

"What did you say?" she frowned. "You *might* get in?"

"So you heard me."

"Yeah," she stepped forward. Not close like she once used to, but close enough for someone to guess that they might be acquaintances at least and not total strangers. "I just don't believe you."

Sykes simply shrugged.

"You've had an epiphany?" she asked.

"Nope."

"Then?"

And another shrug.

"Don't bullshit me, Sykes."

"I'm not," he assured her, "I really am not."

Her eyes narrowed. They were married long enough to know what that look meant. It was never something good.

"You can't be doing this," she shook her head.

"Why not?"

"We have a child, Sykes. Are you out of your mind?"

"I don't see what's wrong," he shrugged.

"You—you *know* what's wrong. We talked about this for *years.*"

Sykes slowly nodded his head. "My child will have a father to be proud of."

"Yeah," she spat, "if you can make it long enough for him to know who you are."

His whole throat tightened from a fast, burning pulse. The twitch came in his hamstrings again.

It's not running away, he told himself, walking past her. *It's running **towards** something I want.*

"Where are you going?"

"Inside," he said, "we're done here, are we not? Take Vulcan and let me know in advance when you're bringing him over."

"Who said we're done?"

He stopped by his door, turning to look at her. "*I did*, for once."

It took a week for Icarus to call him. He was lounging on the sofa, watching TV.

Interviewer: *Sir Dedalus Tarchitec, what is it that you can tell us about your agency's recent success?*

Mr. Tarchitec: *I can tell you a good bit about Icarus. It's more of what you want to know.*

Interviewer: *Well I would like to know—and most people at home watching this will like to know, for sure—what has been the key to your success? You are relatively new in the scene of Crafter Agencies yet you have taken the competition by storm. Your Agency has been key in preventing multiple terrorist attacks on our nation and keeping its citizens safe. What is it that separates you from the likes of Pandora, Prometheus, Zalmoxis,and the sort?*

Mr. Tarchitec: *Well, for starters, unlike Zalmoxis, we are still operating.*

It was only Mr. Tarchitec that laughed. Sykes, at home, chuckled, too.

Mr. Tarchitec: *But that's a very good question and one that I think will get me in some muddied water if I answer, but don't you worry, I will do so nonetheless, even if some feathers might be ruffled. First, I would like to clarify that Icarus' success is **not** recent. That is one key thing I would like to stress. I have been dedicating myself to this agency for over three decades now. Sure, I only managed to officiate it as an agency four years ago this January—but up until that point, I was still toiling away, recruiting the best Crafters and the most brilliant of human minds I could find. We had our successes back then too. They were smaller—more local—dealings, but those are just as important when it comes to* *the people we want to protect. As for differences, there are multiple. Now, I don't want to seem like a sly dog, but at Icarus, only people of similar beliefs are hired.*

Interviewer: *Wouldn't that cause it to turn into an echo-chamber?*

Mr. Tarchitec: *That is something I hear quite often. Sure, that can be an issue, but it hasn't happened yet and I believe there is a simple reason for that: we share a belief but not a way of thinking. Our minds are different, it is our hearts that are the same.*

Interviewer: *And what is that belief, if you don't mind me asking?*

Mr. Tarchitec: *Action is king. You might think it too simple, but it is the truth. It is a well known factoid that great power comes paired with the greatest of responsibilities. Most people—and agencies—can not handle those responsibilities. They get bogged down by what should and shouldn't be done and it delays them. At Icarus, we do nothing of the sort. We act right away.*

Interviewer: *Are you giving your secret away, Mr. Tarchitec?*

Mr. Tarchitec: **hearty laughter* I suppose you can see it that way, but it is not something I worry about and I will tell you why. All these other agencies don't know what it takes to act right away. It can be seen in their involvement rates when compared to ours in the most recent events. I can tell them all of the secrets, but if* *they don't have what it takes to spot the right candidates, they will never be able to achieve what Icarus is achieving.*

Interviewer: *I see, so then—*

Sykes' phone started to ring. He startled out of bed in search of it. He fished with his hand for it, and, following its vibrations, he found it ringing somewhere around his ankles.

He picked it up and answered without even reading who called.

"Hello?" his heart throbbed.

"So are you a Crafter or not?" Montana's voice pierced through his heart, making him deflate.

"I haven't gotten a call from Icarus yet," he mumbled.

"Good," she surely nodded on the other side of the phone. "Then can I bring Vulcan over—are you busy?"

"Were you not going to bring him if I got in?"

"You know the answer to that."

"There's no reason for you to be so harsh about this, Montana."

"I have all the reasons in the world," she spat. "Now can I bring him or not?"

"I mean," he sat up, looking around the place. It was a total mess. He hadn't bothered to clean after himself that whole week, anticipating a call that didn't seem to come. "Of course. I just have to clean up a little bit."

"You've got time," she said, "I'll be there in 20."

"Alright."

"Bye."

She hung up the phone before he could reply.

He took a moment to get his bearings. He then picked up the remote, turned off the TV and got to cleaning.

When Montana got there, the house was as clean as it could get.

"Here he is," she handed the boy over. "I fed him already, so there's no need for you to bother until later in the evening."

"Alright," he nodded, "hey there, buddy," he smiled, letting Vulcan wrap his hands around his neck.

"You look like shit, Sykes."

"Well, thanks. You look great, too."

"What's gotten into you? *Icarus,* I mean, they deal with terrorists and and and...they fight so much and—"

"Montana," he raised a hand. "I didn't get in *yet.* Stop worrying."

"I'm not worried, it's just—" she looked up at him. A breeze hit them both just then, pushing away a wall from between their eyes, allowing them to look into one another for the first time in a long while. Her eyes slid back and forth slowly, growing a little wet. "Just be careful, Sykes, okay?"

A faint smile kissed his lips as he gave her a soft nod.

"And do *wash*, okay? I didn't lie when I said you smell."

"Christ," he chuckled. "Yeah, sure."

She walked back towards her car. Just as she was about to get in, she stopped herself.

"Will you let me know if you get in?" she asked.

"I wouldn't want to disappoint you even more."

"Well, *do*, alright?" she tried for a smile and then got in her car and left.

"That went better than expected, little man," he said as he went back indoors.

Vulcan giggled playfully as his father carried him around the house. He brought him to the living room where he had a large, carpeted playing area for him to enjoy. He put him down and turned on the TV to something colourful for extra distraction.

Sykes sat right next to him, picking up all sorts of toys and shoving them in the baby boy's face in an attempt to play with him, yet his mind was distant. He could only think of Icarus and his reading. So distant, he was, that at first he didn't hear his phone ring.

It took quite a few loops for him to notice it.

"Shoot," he shot to his feet, "just give me a second, bud," and ran towards his room. He picked it up and answered instantly. "Hello?"

"Mr. St. Jane?" Clara's voice came from the other side.

"Yes, hello. That's me."

"Am I calling at a bad time?"

"No, God no. Not at all. What's the matter? When's my Check?"

"There won't be another one."

"What?" his heart sank into his stomach. "But—your policy..."

"You got a reading, Mr. St. Jane."

"I did?" his eyes widened.

"The fact that you are as surprised as you are is quite the concern, I'll have you know, but yes. You did. It was weak, but it was there. You're a Crafter, Mr. St. Jane."

"I...I—woah," he held the phone to his shoulder, looking around for something to sit on. Too restless to pull a chair or walk back, he sat on the edge of the kitchen table.

"I want to ask you one more time," Clara cleared her throat, her tone getting more serious all of a sudden, "are you sure that you hadn't had an epiphany since your last screening?"

"I am certain."

"I see," she suddenly cleared her throat. "You *should* be happy to hear that you meet the minimum requirements to join the agency."

"As a Crafter?"

"Not quite," she sighed. "As a Muffin Man."

"What?"

"Technically, you *are* a Crafter, but your reading came out so low that we could not legally give you combat training or allow you to partake in missions."

"Oh..."

"That is, at least, until we get another reading to ensure that your Crafting capability is truly at the level we have now."

"What do you mean?"

"The Scanner is still broken, Mr. St. Jane. We are just taking the result at face value and giving you a chance. We are...*curious*, to say the least."

Vulcan giggled to the sounds of the TV in the other room.

"What's a Muffin Man?" he drew the conversation back, scratching his head.

"You will be delivering our workers coffee and muffins and mail at times. Menial tasks around the office."

"Will I be cleaning the floors?"

"What? No, we have specific janitors."

"Thank God," he sighed. *At least that.*

"I know this position may not be the *bang* you were talking of, but—"

"I'll take it," he jumped at the occasion.

"Let me finish, Mr. St. Jane," Clara cleared her throat. "As I said, it's not what you might expect, but with another reading, if your capabilities are proven to be higher, we will not hesitate to promote you to an active Crafter Agent, you understand?"

"I understand," he nodded.

"Very well. So—can you come in today?"

Sykes leaned against the doorframe as he watched over his son. Montana appeared as a brief flash before his eyes, but he closed them and shook the image off.

"I'll be there in 15 minutes," he said.

"Perfect. I'll be waiting for you. Oh," she cleared her throat, "will you be bringing your child?"

"How did you know?" he smiled.

"I didn't. I just wanted to make sure. See you soon, Mr. St. Jane."

"Yeah, see you," he took the phone away from his ear.

He held it in his hands, scrolling to *Montana* in his contact list, his finger hovering over the screen.

He pursed his lips, listening to the cartoons playing over in the other room as the smile returned to his face. Sykes placed his phone back in his pocket and hopped off the table.

"Vulcan, boy," he called. The boy turned and smiled at his father. "Big day today, bub. You're in for some child labour."

"I see you're still not wearing a suit," Clara said as she led the way through the halls of the building. Her heels *clicked* with a dull echo in her wake.

Sykes pushed the pram right behind her.

"I wouldn't want the others thinking I'm a genuine co-worker."

"But you are," she turned and smiled, "as of today. Sure, the paperwork still has to be fully filled in and signed, but it might as well be the real thing."

"I didn't know you do tours of the place, too."

"You barely know a thing about Icarus, Mr. St. Jane. You've only been in the screening room until today."

"You are right about that..."

As he continued to walk, he found himself counting his steps. He didn't know whether it was of any use anymore. He wasn't going to get the same number each time he showed up now considering that he got a job there. No one was to know where his feet would take him, what cubicle wanted coffee one day and which wanted it another.

He threw the counting away and tried to listen to Clara as best as he could as she introduced each floor to him and what department it housed.

"You won't remember all that I say," he assured her and he was glad for it, "not for a good while. It's a lot to remember and I understand, but it's better that I walk you around anyway. Now, since you are part of the agency, you have access to our elevator, too. You've seen the card I've been scanning to access it, right?"

"Right," he nodded.

"You'll get one of your own soon. You won't have as many privileges as I or others ranked above you, but you'll be able to visit most floors," she said, scanning her card and calling the lift once more. "Now, we are going somewhere where you wouldn't typically be allowed to go."

"We are?" he asked, "why?"

"I don't know," she admitted. "I was told to bring you there."

He pushed the pram into the elevator. He watched her push the very top button. It had no floor number. It was just a plain, white button.

"Someone high up took an interest in you," she said to him as the elevator kept climbing, "which is both good and bad."

"Why bad?"

"Your every move will be monitored, most likely. Very little space to screw up."

"Lovely," he chuckled.

"Lovely indeed."

The two shared an awkward silence that was broken here and there by a goo or gaa of Vulcan's.

"You won't be a Muffin Man for long, Mr. St. Jane, I can tell you that for certain."

"I won't?"

"No," she shook her head.

"Is that an order from high-up, too?"

"No, it is not. It's just a hunch of my own."

"Ah," he nodded. "Interesting, considering what you told me each time I showed up for a screening."

"I've had a change of heart," she told him. "I can't explain it. Tell me, how high do you want to go?"

"How high?"

"Yes, how high up, Mr. St. Jane. Where do you see yourself at Icarus—let's say, 5 years from now?"

"I don't think of it like that," he shook his head.

"Then how?"

"I just want to go my own way," he said. "I don't care about up and down, left or right. I just need my own path below my own feet. I feel it now, starting to form," he looked at her a moment, to see what she thought. It was then that he first felt her scent; a sweet and fruity perfume. What fruit exactly, he could not tell. "But it's still a long way from leading somewhere.

"I see," she smiled, not with her lips only like before, but with her eyes, too.

Clara chuckled, yet for the first time, she covered her mouth as she did so.

"I still find it hard to believe," she said, "but not as hard as before."

The elevator doors opened just then, cutting their moment short.

"This way," she said.

A large white hall opened up before them. Cold light washed down smoothly over the walls, but the source was uncertain. The air was so sterile that it felt wrong just breathing it; mechanical. Down some distance, voices echoed like lost memories.

"Tell me, Mr. St. Jane, are you good at keeping a secret?"

"It depends what sort of secret."

"Whichever kind," she said, guiding him closer to the voices, "if it has to do with Icarus, you will *have* to be good."

"If it means keeping my job I suppose I *could* make an effort."

"I see," Clara came to a sudden halt, turning towards him. "We won't be going any closer."

Sykes looked around. He saw nothing more than the illuminated white walls of the hall he was already aware of. The voices didn't get that much closer, either.

"Why not?" "That information is not privy to you, I'm afraid."

"Well, alright," he grimaced, shifting on his feet uncomfortably.

"Past that door," she pointed in the very distance, "is the Upper Echelon Six."

"The wh—"

"They are our strongest Crafters here at the agency. Isn't it neat?" she laced her fingers together. "To be able to keep such people hidden from the world?"

"I—"

"They are only called upon in major conflicts. Of those, there have been plenty, I'm afraid. You're aware of The Eastern Bloc Terrors?"

"Y-yes."

"They put an end to that, *yet* nobody knows these people."

"Why—why are you telling me this?"

"Good question," she narrowed her eyes, taking a step closer. She looked up at him, searching. "*Why* am I telling you this? You see, Mr. St. Jane, it's not my choice to do so. It comes from *higher up.*"

"*Oh...*"

"Here at Icarus, there is *very* little choice. Now," she raised her hands to stop any retort, "hear me out. Those people in that room, they had no choice either in the matter of The Eastern

Bloc Terrors. They *had* to go just like I *had* to tell you all of this, *on orders*. You understand?"

Sykes tilted his head, weighed by a great suspicion.

"Everyone at Icarus whole-heartedly aligns with Director Deep's intentions. We *trust* him, so much that we do not question. Our place is to *act*. That is what heroes do, Mr. St. Jane. Even against their own wishes, they will do whatever is necessary for the greater good. *You*, for example, must start wearing a suit."

"Is *that* what this is about?"

"It's about a start. You cannot be thrown into the heat of things. A *suit* is a small first step. Then, as the dominos fall, one day maybe you'll find yourself closer to those doors."

Sykes turned their way. They seemed more distant now, as if no matter how many steps he'd take towards them, he'd never actually reach.

What is that I sense? a voice appeared within his mind. With it, Sykes felt a pair of eyes watching him, yet not from the walls, but rather from inside himself. *Come closer—what makes you stay so far? Consequences? Don't fear—following a heart's will is not a choice, it's an act of heroism. Step closer.*

An itch entered his leg. He let go of the pram and stepped aside. Clara's eyes plastered his broad shoulders.

Fog coated his eyes. It was thick enough to blind him, thick enough to make him freeze on the spot. Once more, paralysed.

His heart started to race. The scent of iron filled his nose, it weighed down on his tongue, also. It made him choke.

As the fog settled over his eyes, he found himself able to peer through it. He was in some other room. It smelt just like how he imagined the outside of an airplane 30000 feet in the air would smell like.

6 figures stood before him, side by side. They called his name. They called to his heart. Yet he could not tell what they were saying.

With a burst, the room went up in flames, engulfing the figures. Burning flesh choked him. The ground quaked and swallowed Sykes up, whilst soundwaves burst his eardrums.

A hand touched his shoulder. He was right back in the white halls.

"We're heading back," Clara told him.

"R-right."

He turned the pram around and pushed it towards the elevator, turning his head, now and then, to take another look at the distant doors, in hopes, perhaps, that the fog would come back so he could make sense of what had just happened.

"So?" she asked as soon as the elevator doors closed.

Sykes shook his head. "I'm a man of choices," he said. "My path's going to be made on nothing but *my* choices."

Clara nodded slowly. "You'll love Gilbert."

"You're not taking me seriously," he clutched the handle of the pram. "I mean it. I cannot be limited by—"

"Saving the world is not a choice, Mr. St. Jane," she cut him short. "Not if that is what you are designed to do. Your feet will move without you making them, your hand will reach out for another just the same. These are not choices."

"What if they are?"

"Then your heart is not in the right place."

The ride down was silent after that. He was brought into a part of the HQ where people were separated in tiny cubicles. Keyboards rattled away from each direction and that. Chairs squeaked and printers beeped and whirred away, forming a constant wave of white noise throughout the office space.

What the hell? he thought, *this is nothing like—*

"Here you are," she waved him into a cubicle. "A little cramped with a pram—"

"Even without it."

"Oh well," she shrugged. "You'll get used to it."

"Will I?" he stepped inside. He was tall enough to look over the cubicle walls. His desk was placed against a northern wall.

Facing it, he saw into an empty cubicle, and, looking past it, in the distance, a giant window opening over the city. If he tried real hard, he could spot Humphrey's Peak vestiges through the skeletal bodies of buildings. "What if I get out of here before I get the chance to settle?

"Surprise us, Mr. St. Jane. We're all for it. But for the time being...

"Sure," he spun, Humphrey's Peak now behind him. To his immediate left stood Clara, right in the entrance. To his right, another empty cubicle. In front, just the same.

Does anyone even work here? Where's all this white noise coming from?

He looked around and could see heads in some cubicles here and there, but for some reason he could not believe them to be real.

"I'll let you settle in," she stepped back. "Don't want to be overbearing."

With her gone, he pulled Vulcan inside so as to not block the narrow corridor. He then sat himself down in a well-chafed office chair. The keyboard caps had seen a great deal of use, too.

His body urged him to feel them, to see if they were still warm with the remnants of the one that was there *before*. He looked around for more clues. He felt the mouse, cheap, plasticky. The desk, too, was not real wood.

Skimping on costs? he wondered, *with the salaries Crafters are paid, I guess you gotta cut things somewhere.*

Still he ran his fingers over the desk until he felt a scratch on the surface. He dragged himself closer and saw two initials etched close to each other—*G + C*—in black-ink pen.

C? Clara? He wondered. *Do we have a romantic on our hands?*

He pulled away, spinning on his chair, laughing at the irony of his fate.

So much time spent trying to get in here, he thought to himself, *so much daydreaming, so much running away from a normal-person life, and still I end up in a cubicle.*

As he spun, he found a calendar pinned to the thin cubicle-wall. He drew closer and saw further proof of someone having been there before him.

A blue pen marked some boxes.

"Let's see," he squinted his eyes, "Kashmere papers, Wednesday, 10:30 a.m. Leave Terry alone," written in bold, each Friday.

Sykes peeled back month after month and these notes repeated themselves on the calendar, jotted down in a blue-inked pen in very neat handwriting.

These can come in handy, he said to himself.

He then turned in search of a pen, marking down the current month with the same notes, just to make it easier to keep track.

Once done, he realised sitting down on a chair wasn't for him, his lower back was already aching.

He sat up, going for a nice old stretch. The cubicle in front of him was still empty, so was the one to his right now.

"Does anybody work here?" he wondered out loud.

"I do," a voice said from behind him. "Need help with any-thing?"

Sykes turned, lowering his arms. The cubicle was occupied, unlike before, by a man leaning back in his chair and swinging just a little as he spun a pen around over his knuckles.

"I'm Gilbert," he said, "you the new guy, right? Our new Muffin Man. Saw you speaking with Clara. Say, you've got a baby with you?"

"I do, yeah."

"Missus not want to take care of it?"

"We're separated."

"Bummer," Gilbert shrugged, suddenly leaning forward on his chair. He bit down on his pen as he typed away for a mo-ment. As soon as he slammed the enter key, he threw himself back, feet-on-desk, taking the pen out of his mouth as he began spinning it over his fingers. "So you need help, yes? Mind if it's me giving you a hand?"

"No, not at all," Sykes sighed, trying to keep up. The man's way of speech seemed way too chaotic. "But it's a bit embarrassing."

"Ah, don't worry about it. We've all been there."

"Really?"

"Nah," he cackled, "some of us skipped right through, but that doesn't matter. Don't be embarrassed—I'm bad with names too. What did you say your name was?"

"I didn't tell you yet."

"See?" Gilbert smiled, tapping his right temple, "I'm just that bad."

"I'm Sykes," he said.

"Sykes," Gilbert nodded, "I'll try remember that. And the baby?"

He turned towards the pram, catching onto its handle, as if it was going to roll away. "Vulcan," he said.

Gilbert shrugged. "Cool. Sykes and Vulcan. Well, listen, man, I won't promise anything. By tomorrow I'll probably forget who you are. Still, nice meeting you."

"Wait, you're going?" Sykes asked, watching the man sit up all of a sudden. "I thought you said you'll help me out."

"3rd floor," Gilbert raised his eyes towards the ceiling. His hands, now, were in his suit pants pockets. "That's my office. This ain't my cubicle."

"It's not?"

"Nah. It's Cole's. You know Cole? No, huh? Well, listen. Cole takes dumps on schedule, and he—"

"Gilbert!"

"Ah, there he is. Hello, Cole, how's things?"

"Gilbert what did you do?" he stepped into the cubicle. He dragged with him the scent of freshly soaped hands.

"Nothing, don't worry about it."

"You saw him, didn't you?" Cole pointed at Sykes as he made it into his cubicle. "Tell me you saw him."

"There was nothing to see," Gilbert shrugged.

Sykes looked at the two men. They stood side by side and couldn't be any further apart from one another. Gilbert was a tall, thin man draped in nonchalance, so much that his eyes drooped with it. There was a wicked sense about his lips, too, from the way they were twisted at the corners.

He was so unbothered that his hair felt it too. It draped down over his shoulders, completely unkempt and brown.

Cole, though, was a ball of stress. His legs were short and chubby and everything from the waist up just grew even more plump. His face was red, either with stress or anger or something else entirely.

His breathing seemed laboured, not at all times, but only when he looked at Gilbert. As he stood there, awaiting an explanation, he ran a hand over his oily, short black hair and then rubbed his thumbs over the tips of all his fingers like an insect.

"Just a few emails, Cole," Gilbert finally shrugged.

"Emails?" Cole's eyes widened, "what emails? I got no emails, Gilbert, what the hell have you been doing at my computer?

"Don't listen to a word this man says, Sykes," Gilbert chuckled as he stepped out of the cubicle, pushing past his rotund friend, "he's drowning in so many emails he can't steer clear of them. But yeah, I lied," he shrugged, "about the email thing. It's not my problem."

"You lied?"

"Kill me for it."

Cole scuttled over to his seat, throwing himself down on it, making it groan with effort. He pulled himself closer to his monitor and squinted his eyes, glancing over some text.

"Ah…" Cole hissed. "You put me down for the get-together. How many times must I tell you?"

"Come on, it'll be fun," Gilbert's eyes rolled in his head so much Sykes thought they might never stop.

"I can't, okay? There'll be alcohol and—"

"No one says you have to drink," Gilbert groaned, "stop being such a child."

"Yeah, right," Cole mumbled, "as if it works like that."

"A lover of drama you are," Gilbert smiled, turning to Sykes. "You come too, Muffin Man."

"Come where?"

"Agency get-together, sorta—it's not official. Who was it, Diego or Santiago that put it together?"

"Diego," Cole muttered.

"Diego, right—I can never tell between those two. Anyway. We're going. You're new, right? You barely know any faces around here. Come and meet everyone, you're sure to remember a few after a night like that."

"I..." Sykes groaned, "I don't know if I can. I mean, I have the baby and everything and—"

"Bring him, too."

Sykes cringed at the prospect.

"You wanted my help, this is it," Gilbert said matter-of-factly.

"I'll see what I can do."

Gilbert nodded. "That's me, then.. I'll head back now before Deep comes to get me."

"Deep?"

"Yeah, Deep," Gilbert looked at him, "the director. Don't tell me you don't even know him."

"I do, I do," Sykes chuckled nervously, "just get him mixed up with Sir Tarchitec."

"You're a funny guy you are, you know that? You make sure to come to that gathering next Saturday. I'll be real upset if you don't—I'm sure Cole would love to have you around, too."

Sykes looked towards Cole. The man did not say a thing. He had his head in his hands, possibly trying to think of an excuse that would get him out of the gathering.

For a moment, Gilbert's eyes fell over the width of Cole's back. A warm pool formed within those eyes, one filled with something clearly foreign to a man like Gilbert. It was there nonetheless. Not for long, though, as he shook himself out of it, looking back at Sykes.

"You can be trusted with keeping this one away from alcohol, right?"

"If I come, sure," Sykes nodded.

"See?" Gilbert raised his hands, "all's good, Cole. All's good. Alright," he stepped backwards down the hall, heading for the elevator. "I'm going up, gents, where my place is. See you around."

Sykes waved him away as the elevator swallowed him up. He then turned to look at Cole. His head was still in his hands

"Don't worry about me," he muttered, "I'll be fine."

"Alright..."

"I'll add you to the group," he added, "so you know what else people are talking."

"Okay, thanks."

"One word of advice..."

"Mhmm?"

"Log out of everything whenever you're away from your computer, Gilbert is sure to snoop around."

"Sure," Sykes nodded. He turned, and for a moment he remained standing before he turned right back. "You need anything?" he asked, "coffee, muffins?"

"What?" Cole lifted his head.

"I'm the Muffin Man, so..."

"Oh...no," Cole shook his head, placing it back in his hands, "unless you can get me out of this gathering."

"I doubt that."

"Yeah..."

Sykes looked around the other cubicles and still found them empty. He then sat himself down on his chair and let his mind wander off for a good while until he came up with a plan.

CHAPTER FOUR

Vulcan slept like a baby the entire day, and, in all honesty, Sykes didn't spend it during much else either. He sat for a good while in his chair listening to the keyboards clacking all around him. It made little sense to him. Why would Crafters be sitting down in cubicles? What was the point of becoming one if you were stuck in an office?

He didn't want to do anything with that. He didn't want to respond to emails or worry about filling in excel sheets. He wanted to be out there, to work towards saving the world first hand.

It simply made no sense. People possessing so much power, capable of so much good—holed up in cubicles. *What even happened to this world? Does everything really need to be put into an office, to be monitored? What happened to being cool and saving the world on your own?*

It's not a choice, the words rang out in his mind. *What does that even mean? I don't buy it.*

There were doubts that rose up in his mind. There were still the words of Ms. Clothos, the idea of lies etching into every part of his life against his will. It was hard to believe things, but he had to shake himself and do so for his own sake.

As he sat there, stretched out in his chair, the question finally came: *When did I become a Crafter?*

He didn't lie when he said that he didn't remember having an epiphany. He told the truth and nothing else, yet somehow, the scanner read that he had achieved the status of a Crafter. He knew nothing of it, not what he was specialised in or what his abilities were.

I didn't even lie to myself about anything yet. I didn't even have the time. What the hell's going on, really? I've got here by some twist of fate. I was so excited about it that I didn't even question it much.

But now the cubicle life dulled the excitement and his bored mind managed to trace its steps back towards what truly mattered: the *how.*

Was it always there? An untapped awakening inside of me that I never knew of? Is that even possible? 31 years and going and just now, **boom**, *I'm a Crafter. That can't be right. Something had to have happened.*

He laced his fingers around the back of his head and leaned back in his chair. Closing his eyes, he decided to think, yet with Vulcan asleep, and with a soothing wash of voices in the distance, Sykes was taken into the land of dreams.

A man floats in the sky. His figure is encircled by the very sun, his whole being shaded. A cape billows down his shoulders. A crowd of people, microphones and cameras in hand, await him on the ground, looking up at him.

He draws near with arms akimbo.

Black coat. White shirt. Black jeans. Black shoes. White cape.

That's him.

His feet touch the ground.

"Sykes! Sykes!" the voices echo. People clamour closer, stepping on top of each other, just to get a look, to catch a whiff, to be able to touch.

Microphones reach for his mouth, cameras flash. He is all smiles.

"How does it feel to save the world? Tell us!"

"Sykes, over here! Let the press know how you're still not wearing a suit!"

"What's next for you, Sykes, now that the world is free of tyranny?"

"What's next?" Sykes' smile drops. He looks at the strange face that asked the question. He cannot tell man from woman. "I...I never thought that far."

"You haven't thought that far? You're the world's hero! You put Icarus on your back! How can you say such a thing!"

"Yes how? Sykes elaborate, please, please!"

Cameras flash some more, microphones get closer. Sykes draws back, but his feet are sinking into the ground.

"Sykes, over here!" a voice calls from the right and he looks. "Tell us who did you do this all for."

"What?" Sykes asked.

"Was it to save the world or was it for yourself?"

"Huh?"

"Did you do it for a greater good or did you do it for th—"

BANG!

The building to his right exploded.

BANG!

To the left was the next, no time to react.

BANG!

BANG!

BANG!

BANG!

BANG!

BANG!   ***BANG!***

BANG!

BANG!

One after the other they come. The people scatter, running and screaming. Microphones and cameras drop to the ground as the world goes out with a ***BANG!*** all around him.

There's only one left with him as he sinks into the ground. It is Vulcan, standing on two feet, holding a microphone.

"Who did you do it for, Pop?" Vulcan asks.

Yet before Sykes can think to answer, he startles back awake.

His eyes were curtained with sleep as he stood up. He stretched once more and checked the clock on the wall. *16:32.*

Cole was not in his cubicle. A blonde haired woman was the one in the front.

"Hey," he called to her.

She turned and smiled.

"Hey."

Her left eye was blue, the right green.

"I'm Sykes," he said, "the new Muffin Man. You need any-thing?"

"Oh," she nodded. She had a hunch about her that made it seem like a great deal of effort to make a single move. "I've already got my coffee, thanks. I'm Gina, by the way."

"Well, Gina, if you need anything," he tried to sound genuine, but sleep still plagued his voice, "pop your head over and I'll see what I can do."

"Will do, thanks."

As he sat back down, he heard Cole's laboured breathing enter his own cubicle. Once more, he carried the scent of fresh-ly-washed hands with him. Picking up a pen, Sykes rolled to the calendar and wrote:

Cole poop? 16:32

As he rolled back towards the computer that he still didn't bother to turn on, Vulcan started to wake up.

"Hey there, buddy," Sykes whispered, not wanting to be a nuisance, "you're awake, are you? We're still at work, so don't go crazy on me, alright?"

The boy looked at him with glee and wonder in his eyes.

"Mr. St. Jane?"

Sykes straightened right up, turning around. Clara was stand-ing at the entrance to his cubicle.

"Oh, Clara, hello."

"How are things working out for you? Busy day?"

"Not really, no," he admitted.

"Did you meet anyone, remember any names?"

"Met Gilbert," Sykes nodded, "*great* character."

"So it goes."

"Cole, too, over yonder," he points, "and Gina. No one else, really."

Clara inspected him for a moment. "Come with me for a second, won't you?"

Sykes looked into the pram first to check that Vulcan was still asleep before he agreed.

"What?"

"What did you think of Gilbert?" she asked, walking him down the corridor. "Did you like him?"

"He was a bit *loose* for my taste, but, I mean," he shrugged, "he was fine."

"Interesting. *Loose*, huh?"

"Yeah, *loose*."

"I see," she smiled, coming to a stop. "Well, Sykes, I have a task for you. The first of many."

My first task at Icarus, I wonder what—

"Could you go around cubicle to cubicle and collect all of the trash? Make sure to recycle them properly, the big bins are just down in the basement. If you take the elevator you can't miss them."

The more she spoke and he listened, the more he deflated.

"Bins?"

"Yes, bins," she nodded, "did I say something wrong?"

"No, I just—" he wanted to go on, but then, remembering what his position entailed, he shook his head, "nevermind. I'll do it, yeah."

"Want me to stay with Vulcan?"

"You'll do that?" He raised his brow. "For real?"

"I don't see what the problem is, as long as you don't mind. I'm done for the day."

"Well," he made his way back to his cubicle, followed by her. He chewed on his bottom lip, his eyes fixated somewhere distant.

"It won't be long," she assured him, "I'm sure you'll make quick work of it."

"Alright," he sighed, convinced, "here," he handed her a pacifier from a pram-pocket, "if he wakes up just pop this in his mouth. He'll behave."

"Will do."

Fucking bins, man, really?

Collecting trash was nothing but tedious.

This is not what I dreamt of at all. If this is what my work days will look like from now on, where will I even have space to show what I can do?

He had to think of a way up. Weighed down by leaking trash-bags was definitely not it.

The elevator *dinged* as its doors opened into a small room. Grey faience plastered the walls and a white light flickered as if out of a horror movie. He wasn't one to be irked by such things, so he walked towards another door, pulled it open with his elbow, finding himself inside of the underground parking lot.

From the moment he got there, the hairs on his back raised and a net of goosebumps spread over him. He looked over his shoulder, trying to see if anyone else was there with him.

He spotted a camera in the corner. At first glance, nothing appeared strange, but then he noticed that the cables were ripped right out of it.

Huh...

Sykes walked around in search of the dumping lot. Every few steps he looked over his shoulder yet again. He couldn't shake the feeling that a set of eyes hooked itself to the back of his head.

He walked the whole length and saw no clear indicator. Turning on his feet, he noticed the long line of liquid which leaked out of one of the bags, trailing behind him.

With a shiver of disgust, he turned his head sideways. That's when he noticed two people inside of a black BMW.

With no other options, he went to ask them for directions. As he approached, he noticed that they were suited up. White was the colour of choice, black that of the ties.

Yet that was not the most bizarre thing of all. At first, the darkness of the car made it hard to see, but now, right by the hood, he noticed they were wearing masks; *stone masks.*

Fashion statement? He wondered, *or are we hiding something? What's the deal?*

He got a little closer, right next to the passenger side window, when he noticed that they were stone masks, too. The one in the passenger seat appeared to be a mask depicting a male. The mouth hole was gaped and the nose twisted and squashed. The cheeks seemed to be made out of noodles, twisted and twirled, a pattern that followed along on the rest of his face. There was a deep, contorted frown on the brow and the eye-holes were barely big enough to be able to see through. The mask seemed to extend up and past the forehead, covering the top of the head, too, with a stoney slicked-back hair.

The driver had a much more feminine mask. Its features were prettier and less aggressive, yet they were still stoney and angular, adorning a hard-set nose and sharp cheekbones. The hair was all engraved curls, falling over the forehead in bangs and some strands on the side of the mask. In addition, lines resembling circuitry streaked her face in random intervals, cutting through the cheeks vertically.

What sort of shit is this? Halloween's nowhere close, is it?

The masked figures had enough of him standing there and rolled down the passenger side window.

"Can we help?" the presumed woman leaned over and asked.

"Uhm...who are you?"

The two figures exchanged a brief glance.

"Comicon nearby?" he chuckled nervously. The figures were silent. "Forget that," Sykes lifted the bags. "Got any idea where I can dump these? I'm new here."

Another look, a little longer. It gave him some time to think.

"Well?" he asked after a while. "These are starting to stink and—"

The woman twisted in her seat, extending her arm. For some reason, Sykes couldn't help but follow its entire span, from the top, all the way down towards her pointed finger, directing him behind their car.

"And then you take a right," the man said in her stead, catching Sykes off guard. His voice, too, was oddly muffled by something mechanical, unlike the woman's.

Sykes' eyes were still on the woman's arm. He noticed that from right below her sleeve, a golden-tinged light flashed in his eye. He tried to get a better look, yet the woman, seemingly catching on, quickly put her arm away and drew the window up.

"Thanks," he nodded, scurrying away before he got into trouble.

As he followed her directions, he put two and two together.

*They're dressed in suits, they know where the trash is. They **must** be working here, right? But they're different suits. Everyone at Icarus wears beige suits and burgundy ties. Maybe...no. No shot.*

His mind raced briefly to the Upper Six, but he found it hard to conceive.

It's a possibility, though, he found himself thinking as he dumped the bags. As he did, he heard the engine of a car turning on in the distance, its sound growing more and more quiet as time passed.

Once he stepped out of the dumping spot, the car was gone, as he had expected.

Suppose I shouldn't have seen them, he sighed. Yet as he made his way back, he realised that the feeling of being watched hadn't gone away. He paced around a bit more, checking for cameras, yet the only one he found was the one with its ripped chords in that first corner.

In his search, he came upon many cars still parked. It was nearing the end of the workday, yet still, there was barely a sign of anyone leaving. Most cars did not stand out. Even with an upper range in salaries, Crafters appeared to be reserved people when it came to their vehicles of choice.

All except for one and Sykes was standing right by it now, admiring it.

A 1969 Chevrolet Corvette ZL-1, matte black.

"Christ," he brought his forehead close to the window to look inside, "this is a beauty."

"Tell me about it," Gilbert's voice echoed over the parking lot.

"Shit, man. Say something. How long were you there for?"

Gilbert shrugged. "Just got here. Neat car, eh?"

"It's cool as hell," Sykes pointed.

"Sticks out a little too much, don't you think?"

"Nah, man, what? This is *the* car to have," Sykes smiled.

"You lit up like a bulb," Gilbert placed a cigarette in his mouth. "You a car guy?"

"Not at all. I just like the way some look."

"This one?" Gilbert nodded towards it.

"Top of the class stuff."

"I see," he inhaled. "What do you drive?"

"Nothing. I take the cab."

"Jeesh. Get yourself a car, man," Gilbert walked away. "And get away from this one. I bet the fucker's that got a car like that don't want anyone breathing near it."

"Right," Sykes nodded, "yeah.

"By the way," Gilbert cleared his throat. "Clara's looking for you."

"Is she? Shit, alright. Good seeing you."

"Yeah," Gilbert mumbled. "Good."

Once back in the elevator, the feeling of being watched had washed away from him.

Clara was rocking the pram back and forth when he returned to his cubicle.

"I'm here," Sykes panted. "What do you need from me?"

"*Need* from you?"

"Well, Gilbert said—" he stopped, taking a deep breath as he realised that he had played him. "Nevermind," he sighed. "How was Vulcan? Caused you any headaches?"

"None at all, actually. He's a well behaved boy."

"Takes after his mother."

"Took me just a second to figure that out," she uncrossed her legs, standing up.

"Meaning what?"

"Meaning nothing," she stepped out of the cubicle.

"You know, he's really bad with strangers. I don't know what it is but he just sorta…loses his cool, like he can sense it's not me or his mother around."

"Really?"

"Yeah. Are you sure he didn't cause a scene?"

"I'm sure, Mr. St. Jane."

"Woah, well," he looked confused, "I guess he likes you or something. You've got a kid of your own?"

Well on her way out, Clara stopped, anchored by the question. She took a deep breath and in that same motion let out an *I do* heavier than the world itself.

"C-cool," Sykes said.

And they left it at that.

The watchful gaze still pressed itself against Sykes' back the following day as he made it to the office.

He was alone this time, so he was less mindful of it, but it pressed heavily onto him from the moment he stepped out of the cab. It followed him into the building and towards his cubicle, where he found a mail-delivery trolley right by his cubicle.

He stepped on past it and settled into his rat-cage, turning on the computer (for no reason) and checking his calendar.

What's come over me? He wondered, *no one's out to get you, bud. Stop freaking out.*

He turned to his calendar and moved the marking square over to *Wednesday* and then leaned back in his chair.

Who have I irked? Clara did mention that she was given orders from higher up about me. Mr. Deep? Surely not...or maybe...God...a guy like me? For what? Be real.

He thought back to the voice he heard when he neared the Upper Six Room. It called to him then.

Maybe that?

Yet he hadn't felt the eyes upon his back then. It was someone else.

Someone I met between that. Gilbert? Cole? What for?

Unable to piece it all together in that moment, he was reminded of the mail trolley.

He poked his head out of his cubicle, looking left, right, to see if someone was coming for it. He even scanned each parcel to see if any belonged to him; nothing.

"Cole," he stood up, looking into the other cubicle.

"Yes?"

"The mail, is it *my* job?"

"Oh, right, yes," he nodded, "Clara told me to let you know, but I forgot all about it. I already took mine," he lifted two envelopes from his desk, "so there's no need to look for mine."

"Cool, then. I'll take them out."

He got behind the trolley and started pushing around the whole building, going from cubicle to cubicle, meeting new faces.

"You the new Muffin Man?" they'd ask him and he'd say *yeah that's me* and nod at them and then they'd tell him. "Could you bring me a coffee?"

Half-way through he realised he delivered more coffees than he did mail.

He pushed on and checked the clocks on the wall each time he straightened his back. At once it was 9 am and then 9:04 and then somehow 10:26 a.m and there were still parcels to be passed around.

It was then that he remembered the marking on the calendar. He had four minutes to find the cubicle. As he ran around, people asked for coffee and tea and biscuits and their mail but he told them *later later later* and at times even asked *where's Kashmere? Kashmere? Where's she?* and nobody really answered him as he was in an awful rush, until, finally, he ran through all the cubicles on that floor and found her thrown in some corner.

Her cubicle wasn't like his own. She had a L-shaped sofa pressed against the wall and lounged on it as she ran her fingers over a large canvas, colour seeping out of them.

As he came to a stop, his back was hunched as he panted.

10:30, the clock said.

"Kashmere?" he asked.

"That's me!"

"I think I have to give you some papers."

"Oooh...papers," she smiled, turning around in her stool. "Where are they?" she looked at him with a set of golden eyes. Her dark afro was large, expanding like the branches of a tree, filling up the cubicle.

"That's the thing. I don't know. The previous Muffin Man—"

"Grigory?"

"Grigory, yes," he nodded.

"How mindful of him," she stood up, crouching next to the trolley, "they are here, don't worry. Just this," she picked it up from the bottom tray. "Thanks."

He turned and left and—

"Dope sideburns," she called from behind him, yet he was too taken aback by how young she was to be in a cubicle to respond in any way.

After that, he returned to the cubicles he skipped over just to get in time to Kashmere's own and delivered their mail and other office-needs.

Once he was done with them all, he realised he still had some left.

3rd floor, it said on them, and that's where he went.

He pushed the trolley to the elevator, then inside, and then up he went.

The atmosphere on the 3rd floor was completely different. He found himself staring down a spacious hall with glass-walled offices flanking it on each side.

No privacy whatsoever, Sykes thought, *strange.*

On the glass doors, black plaques were glued with names engraved into them. At the very end of the long corridor was a kitchen area, or so it seemed.

He paced up, looking side to side and checking the names of his mail and trying to match them with the names on the plaques until he found the office of a Terry Finster.

He pulled the trolley aside, holding the envelope. The large man noticed him before he even knocked, and nodded at him to come in.

"For me?" his voice was thick with accent.

"Yes sir."

"Don't call me sir," he said. "I ain't above you in no way shape or form. We're both men of equal value."

"It's out of respect."

"You can respect a man without calling him sir," Terry said, pushing away from his desk. He rested his hands on his knees as he looked at Sykes. "You can respect *anything* in your own kind of way, it don't have to be like everyone else says."

"True that," Sykes smiled.

"It's why you're not wearing a suit, right?" Terry asked. "Not *your style*, I imagine?"

"Bang on."

"Thought as much. Will be great to see just how long you get on before you fall in line with the others, young man."

"I wouldn't call myself young. My knees hurt when I stand up."

"You think that's what defines a man's youth, how his body feels?"

"I mean, biologically—"

"Who gives a good goddamn about *biologically?*" Terry threw the envelope on his desk. "We're talking about a man's soul. If you're young there then you're young everywhere, don't matter no way or another how old you are."

"Alright."

"You strike me as that."

"Alright," Sykes repeated, not knowing where the conversation was going.

"A lot of men watch their youth wilt away, you hear me? They watch it and they're all a sad bunch after. Better to go out with it clenched between your teeth, eh?"

Sykes looked at the man. He knew why, and, even so, he couldn't stop himself from muttering:

"Go out with a *bang*."

"That's it right there! You're a bright young mind you are and you know what?"

"What?"

"It's a goddamn pity you're nothing but a Muffin Man. With dreams like that you've got to be something else entirely. There's no *bang* to a man delivering mail and fetching muffins."

"I mean—"

"Now don't be selling me no bull that there is *bang* to all sorts of men. That's chickenshit and we both know it. Here, listen, how about it," he pulled his chair close to the glass wall, "see that corner over there," he pointed far in the distance, "how about you *bang* on out of here and fetch me a coffee and three sugar packets?"

"3?"

"Yeah, 3."

"Goddamn," Sykes muttered, stepping out of the office.

His mind was numb as he stepped towards the distant kitchen area, finding the coffee machine. It whirred and hummed and gurgled so loudly that it took the numbness away from his mind.

What the hell was he on about in there? What's he talking like that for?

His eyes drifted off, anchoring to a non-existent point in the distance.

But he's right, he sighed as the machine stopped.

"Thanks," Terry said as soon as he was back, "you move quick. You're a good man. Pity is all, about that whole *bang* thing."

"I don't need pity," Sykes said, "thanks very much."

Terry's face suddenly tightened. He scanned Sykes as he pulled out of the office without a word, pushing away at the trolley.

"Good," Terry whispered, "very good."

There were 3 more envelopes left in the trolley. All 3 of them belonged to Gilbert. Before he could even read the names, Sykes had a suspicion as to which office was his.

Amongst the transparent glass walls, there was one in particular that was clouded by thick, rolling smoke.

As he approached it, his whole body seemed to be weighed down. For some odd reason, he felt the need to turn and look over his shoulder, uncertain of himself.

Get your shit together. No one's watching you. Come on.

He pulled the trolley close, checked the embossed name, picked up the three envelopes and knocked.

"Very brave of you to show your face here," Gilbert called through the smoke.

"Just some mail."

"Oh yeah. Took a while. Come in."

Nothing could be seen inside. As Sykes pushed the door, the smoke spilled out. It was warm and thick and it rushed up his lungs, making him choke.

"Don't be a rookie, Sykes. Took you a while to get to me. Anyone keep you occupied?"

"Terry."

"Mouthin' off on ya?"

"Sure as hell he did, yeah," Sykes chuckled.

"That's just Terry. Here, give those over."

"I can't see where."

Gilbert suddenly appeared from within the smoke. He had a cigar in his mouth, half-way smoked, the end of it red as he took another drag.

He reached for envelopes and threw them onto his desk.

"Is this the part where you ask me to get you coffee?" Sykes asked.

"Bingo," Gilbert finger-gunned him.

Sykes groaned as he took two steps back, ready to go out the door when Gilbert stopped him.

"I ain't getting my coffee from there. That thing's trash, it'll rust your insides. Why do you think everyone 'round here's so stiff?"

"Then where?"

"I'll take you along," he said, walking back into the smoke and coming out without his cigar anymore. "Let's go."

"What about—"

"Don't you worry about nothing. Just come."

Gilbert drove the very 1969 Chevrolet Corvette ZL-1 that Sykes gawked over the other day. The damn thing purred like a cat in heat with the windows up, but it was only when Gilbert rolled his down to throw out his cigarette that Sykes could hear the engine's roar, like a lost beast from another world, as they sped down the streets of Chives Dale, leaving behind the high-rises.

"We're going pretty far," Sykes said.

"Sure we are."

Silence choked their dry necks as the car drove on. It was a smooth ride as all signs of civilization bar the road they were on disappeared, leaving space for Humphrey's Peak to rise up out of the ground and loom over them.

From the distance the mountains looked blue with the snow sprinkled over their caps like salt. The road was a mighty snake, coiling each way and that, yet all the same Gilbert never slowed the car. He didn't give the damn thing a break. Sykes was thrown about in his seat, hitting against the door as he struggled to keep himself in one place.

The whole way, Gilbert lit 7 cigarettes. He smoked them all in one drag and then flicked them out the window, all whilst speeding.

Sykes knew better than to ask anymore questions, so he waited for the car to stop and stop it did. They were ways off the main road. They were in the middle of a field.

"Out," Gilbert said, and out Sykes went.

The earth was the colour of the sun but it gave off no heat. There was only a desolate cold that ran up into his bones as he slammed the door shut. Sykes looked around and saw nothing.

"Doubt we'll get a coffee here, Gilbert," he said, walking around the hood of the car. He stopped as soon as he saw Gilbert pointing a finger-gun at him.

"There's no coffee, Sykes."

"Could tell as much, officer," Sykes put up his hands. "What am I being detained for?"

"I'm not joking around."

"Sure you aren't," Sykes smiled, "so what if I—" he suddenly pointed two finger guns at Gilbert, but before he could even blink, a red, hot beam shot out of Gilbert's finger, passing right by his ear with such heat that he felt the skin scorch without it even being touched.

Sykes froze on the spot.

"What the hell?!" Sykes roared, "what the hell was that?!" he brought his hand to his ear, holding it, looking back where the beam hit the ground. There was a hole burned right on through, going God-knows how deep. "What's going on?!"

"You tell me, Sykes."

"Tell you what? There's nothing to tell you!"

"Wouldn't you think it odd?" he asked.

"Think what odd? What the hell are you talking about?"

"Day 1: Ms. Clothos goes on TV and makes that announcement. The whole world comes to a stop and everyone's scratching their heads about Crafters."

"I was just as confused."

"Immediately after, *Zalmoxis* ceases to exist. All of its Crafters—poof, gone."

"I...I didn't know that—that was never—"

Another red beam shot by, this one a little closer. Sykes shut up.

"*Day 2*," Gilbert continues, "Sykes St. Jane, a nobody, applies for the 7th time at our agency. All the cards were stacked against him, considering, of course, that he was a nobody. There was no reason to believe that from attempt 6th to attempt 7th, that he had become somebody, was there? What are the odds?"

Sykes said nothing. A gust of wind simply blew by, unencumbered by the lack of trees, and so it howled with all of its might, rattling Sykes and making him stumble, falling against the hood of the car.

Gilbert's fingers followed him.

"But not only did our nobody become somebody, but he blew the fuse off our scanner. Power went out in the whole damn building and no place else on the entire block. Next thing you know, you're a Crafter; a weak one, presumably, but I don't buy it. Show me your Log, Sykes."

"I...I don't know how to conjure it."

"Is that what they told you to say?" Gilbert asked.

"Who!? Who told me?! Are you crazy, man? I have no clue what you're talking about."

"Are you claiming you're a nobody?"

"Y—" Sykes stopped himself.

"That's what I thought. Show me your Log, Sykes. Or is that altered as well? Does it show you're as weak a Crafter as you claim to be?"

Sykes thought he would shake like a wet dog in such a moment. He found himself oddly still, as if he was dead already.

"I...I don't know how to conjure my Log. I...I've never taken it out before."

"It's simple," Gilbert raised his free hand, flicking two of his fingers as if flipping over the page of a book.

A black book materialised before him. It floated in the air, no writing engraved on the covers. Thick chains dropped down from all covers, swaying in its floating presence.

"Look," Gilbert flicked again, turning the Log around to face. "That's how you do it. Come on. If you've got nothing to hide, you'll let me read it, right? Nothing to hide."

"Gilbert, please, I—"

"Your Craft, it's strength, your abilities. Why hide them? We work for the same Agency, don't we? We're supposed to trust each other with this sort of information."

"Trust?" Sykes scoffed. "Is this *trust* to you?"

"It's *establishing* it."

"God," shuddered Sykes, "Gilbert, I swear—"

Gilbert flicked once more, a red beam shooting by Sykes' other ear.

"DO. IT."

Sykes mimicked the movements. His Log materialised as Gilbert had expected. The problem, though, was another.

"It's white, huh?" Gilbert's eyes narrowed. "What does that mean, Sykes? Why is it white?"

"What? I...I don't know, I—"

"Every goddamn Crafter Log is black, motherfucker. *Why* is it white? *Who* are you?"

Sykes shook his head, not knowing what to say. "You've got precisely 2 seconds to open your fucking mouth."

"I DON'T KNOW!" Sykes roared. "I DON'T KNOW WHO I AM!"

"That's better," Gilbert nodded. "*More.*"

"I don't know, alright? I don't know who you want me to be. I...I am Sykes St. Jane. I swear it to you! I have a child, Vulcan St. Jane, and—and, God—a wife, I mean, *had* a wife, Montana St. Jane. My father...well, I have an adoptive father—or had, and then my biological but—listen, man, do you really want to know my goddamn roots?"

"I just want to know the story," Gilbert said, "beginning to end."

"*What* story?"

"Who are the Masks, Sykes?" Gilbert gritted. "You met them in the parking lot."

"Wh—what?" Sykes chuckled. "This...this is about *that*?"

"You don't deny it?"

"I...I don't. I have no clue who they are. I...I just needed directions to throw the trash and—hold on," he just realised, "it was *you*? You were watching me this whole time?"

"So you picked up on that? *Well done,*" he spat, "but it's too late now. You should've been more careful."

"Careful about what? I swear I don't know who they are."

"You really aren't going to co-operate, are you?"

Sykes looked at him, not knowing what to say. His mouth opened multiple times but nothing came out, not until the very end, when he saw the look in Gilbert's eyes.

"Are you going to kill me?" Sykes asked. "Is that why we're out here?"

"When did you figure it out?"

"Just...just now."

"Well, I made up my mind back in the office," Gilbert said.

"I..."

"Don't bother with excuses, there's no—"

"I'm not letting you," Sykes muttered.

"Sure as fuck try to stop me," Gilbert smiled. "I'd love to see you try."

As if given a command, Sykes rolled over the hood and away from Gilbert, putting the car between the two of them.

"You fuck," Gilbert hissed, losing track of Sykes all together. He looked through the windows to try and spot him, but he couldn't see him on the other side.

Gilbert mumbled, lowering his hand as he made it towards the other end of the car.

Sykes wasn't there.

"Where the hell did you go?" he asked. "Do you vanish? Is that your Craft? Are you some Invisible Man?"

Gilbert slowly stepped along the side of his car, coming to a stop, peering inside just to make sure. Before he could take his eyes away, two hands clutched at his ankles, yanking his legs from beneath him.

He thudded against the ground, rattled. Sykes came out from underneath the car, straddling him with his knees as he held down both his arms by the wrist, allowing Gilbert's hands no mobility.

"Well, shi—" Gilbert groaned, but then Sykes' headbutted him straight in the nose, cracking it.

Thick blood gushed out.

Another headbutt came, smushing his nose even more.

Sykes' whole body heaved as he stared down into Gilbert's blood-splattered face.

What the hell? He thought to himself, tears erupting out of his red eyes, *what the actual hell?*

"I believed you the first headbutt," Gilbert murmured. "There wasn't a need for a second."

"You...you tried to kill me!"

"Nah," Gilbert turned his head, spitting some blood that pooled up in his mouth against the floor. "Was just a test."

"What for? Why like that?!"

"I'm an eccentric man, so I've been told," Gilbert flashed him a bloodied smile. "Now will you let me smoke a cig?"

The two sat on the car's hood, watching the distant peaks, like some god awful pyramids, green and white and blue and black, crooked but taller than anything man's ever accomplished.

Smoke billowed out of Gilbert's mouth; a curtain falling in reverse over his eyes, then away and gone.

"I was born right here," Gilbert suddenly said.

"What, like in Chives Dale?"

"No. Right on this goddamn spot, right here where we are."

"In a field?"

"Many men were born here," he stared out into the distance as he spoke. It was unclear whether he still watched the mountains or if his eyes saw something beyond them, something only he could see. "I'm told my grandpops was the first to be born here but I'm sure there were many more before and there's many more to come after. You were born here, too."

"Is that just tobacco?" Sykes asked.

Gilbert shook his head. He allowed a chuckle to escape his lips; Sykes deserved that much.

"The moment you grabbed my ankles and pulled the world from beneath me, that's when you were born."

"My mother would tell you otherwise."

"Yeah, wouldn't they all?"

Gilbert looked at the stub of his cigarette, burning its last. He flicked it in the distance and then lit another.

"You sure you don't want one?" Gilbert asked.

"Stop tempting me."

"Alright. Well," he sighed, "listen. The way I see it, a man's born twice but can only die once. So at the end of his life, he's bound to come out on top."

"How's that?"

"Two minus one gives you a positive still, it's as simple as that. You get forced out your mother, that's one. Then, like you this afternoon, right down here on this damn field, you became something. I like to call it a man. You," he pointed, "call it whatever the hell you want, it makes no difference. But something came on fire inside of you, I'm sure of it. It was for the first time, too. I could see it on your face."

"So that makes two?" Sykes asked. "At death's door, born out of fire—out of anger?"

"I wouldn't call it anger."

"It felt that way."

CHAPTER FIVE

Gilbert shrugged. "Sure, I guess. But I'd call it something else."

"What?"

"I don't know. Not anger," he said. "But that don't matter now. What matters is what you choose from now on. You either go back to the man you were, or you keep on stoking the flames. Now one of these choices is going to make your dear momma upset, and it ain't the one you're thinking about. So," he watched another cigarette go as he stepped off the hood. "You tell me why you threw yourself underneath my car and we're driving back."

"I took a chance," Sykes said.

"A chance, eh?"

"I said to myself, who's gonna ruin a damn nice car over a nobody?"

"Damn right."

3:33 pm, Thursday, Clara showed up with a bouquet of flowers.

"Sykes," she called, making him jump, "Mind coming with me?"

"Huh, what?" he shuddered, his mind latched onto the previous day. "Where?"

"To pay our respects."

Sykes was sitting in the front seat as Clara drove. He was starting to feel a little bit of deja vu, and, if it hadn't been for Cole sitting in the back, or the trunk full of flower bouquets, he would've more than likely never gotten in the car, not after what happened with Gilbert.

"Who are we paying our respects to?" Sykes let the question out in the car.

The silence that followed let him know that it was a much heavier question than he had given it credit.

"Our previous Muffin Man," Clara said.

"Oh…"

"Oh…is right," Cole called from the back.

The rest of the journey was silent.

"His family did not want him buried in our Agency Cemetery," Clara told him as they walked down the muddy path. "They were Non-Crafters."

She needn't say more.

Sykes struggled to walk, his arms filled with bouquets of all sorts. Cole, behind him, carried just as many, yet he was well better off, as was Clara with her own load.

They came to a stop in front of a drab gravestone.

"Place them down nicely," she said, "all around."

The three of them did so in silence for an upward of 15 minutes, all until the gravestone seemed to spring back to life with all of the colourful flowers around it.

Sykes and Clara stood back as Cole hung his head low, quietly sobbing to himself.

"How often do you do this?"

"Every month on the 21st," she told him. "That's when we lost him."

"Aha."

"You will have to do it from now on," she sighed. "But do let me know if it's too much to ask. We've never had this occur before, so it's new, even for us."

"It's fine with me. You two can come along as well, or hell, anyone for that matter. There's a lot of flowers here. People must've loved him."

"They did, yeah. He was great."

"My condolences," Sykes murmured.

Clara nodded, taking them in.

Without a word, Cole stepped away. Sykes turned to go after him, yet Clara caught his hand and stopped him. Her fingers were warm and a little sweaty even though it was quite chilly outside.

"Let him," she whispered.

"Alright."

"He's still really affected."

"They must've been close."

"You can't even imagine," she shook her head. "But Cole is like that with everyone. He loves us all at Icarus. There's not a single heart as big as his."

"Doesn't feel like he's like that with me."

Clara shrugged. "Maybe an adverse effect, who knows. I'm sure it's temporary. He'll warm up to you. Do you mind if I keep holding your hand?"

"What?" Sykes asked, "oh...I didn't even notice you never let go. No, I don't mind."

"Thanks."

She clutched a little tighter at it as her eyes latched onto Grigory's gravestone. Her eyes watered and he allowed for the wind to speak all the words that needed to be spoken in that moment.

Sykes looked over the other gravestones. They all belonged to Non-Crafters. He could tell from the fact that there were no guards pacing up and down the cemetery, trying to protect the graves from getting desecrated.

How strange, he thought, *to dedicate yourself towards humanity's well-being and still to be treated like crap, even in death.*

It always baffled him how someone could look at a Crafter and think anything but *good* things. They unlocked the human mind's true potential, what was there to hate? That's the word people used *hate*, yet Sykes never thought it was quite right. *Envy* fit a lot better.

He never understood, not until some days back when Ms. Clothos' statement came out and shook the world. For a moment, he found himself surrounded in hate, too.

"How come there weren't flowers here when we came?" Sykes asked, breaking the silence.

"His parents clear them out. They want nothing to do with us."

"Not even flowers?"

"Not even," she shook her head.

"You'd think they'd leave some of their own, at least."

"You'd think, yeah, but no," she sighed. "They say they loved their son, but not a day went by without Grigory cracking some joke about how they hated him."

"That's the thing about jokes, you crack them enough times they might spill out the truth."

"Yeah," she nodded. "I don't know, it's just strange to me."

"I get it," he shrugged. "People can be strange like that."

"Can they really?"

"Yeah, I mean...my wife," he said, and then, for some reason, grew increasingly aware of Clara's hand in his, "my *ex-wife*," he cleared his throat, "she's not keen on Crafters, either. Big reason why we separated."

"Really?"

"Well, there were other things. You know how it is with divorce, it's not just one issue, it's an...amalgamation. *Crafting* itself was one *big* thing, but it wasn't the *biggest*."

"What was?"

"My blind ambitions," he sighed.

"Ah," she nodded, "that checks out."

He turned to her, narrowing his eyes. "Alright, that's it. Hand-holding privileges revoked."

"Hey!" she pouted, "I wasn't done!"

"If you want to hold it you've got to trade sob-stories."

"What?"

"Come on. What ails you? I've told you about my ex-wife, you tell me something about you. It's fair game. Your parents? Husband? Friends? Something's gotta give."

Clara shook her head. "My parents support what I do. I'm not married—thank God—and all my friends work at Icarus. There," she smiled, catching hold of his hand once more. "Now let me be at peace."

He looked at her as she closed her eyes, pointing their darkness into the ground.

"There are some things," she started, "but I don't think I'm quite ready to talk about them."

"Sure," he said, squeezing her hand in return. "No worries."

Sykes sat by the edge of Vulcan's cot, completely drained. He didn't understand where the fatigue was coming from. He felt the vestiges of a body-ache tingling at his muscles, yet from *what* he couldn't tell.

He leaned against the cot, arms crossed and pressed against it as he placed his head down on it.

Office work busts your fucking balls.

It was late into the night, the light of the moon spilling in. The baby's breaths were soft and quiet, as were Sykes' thoughts.

He still couldn't figure out how he got in. He did not experience an epiphany, yet somehow…

Why is it white? was a good enough question. Gilbert didn't bring it up again. Not on the way back, not since.

He had analysed his Log book as soon as he had gotten home that day, yet quickly realised that he could not read the writing within it. It was in a completely different script than what he was used to.

What the hell's going on with me? Things are just **happening** *and I have no clue why or how.*

With a yawn and the soothing *coos* of his boy by his ear, he drifted off into sleep.

He awakes in his bed. His eyes are open but he cannot tell whether it is day or night. A baby's cry assaults him from the right. It's louder than what he's used to hearing.

He sits up; looks around. It is dark, yet somehow, as he looks out of the window, a blinding light rushes back at him. It does not spill into the room, it stays outside, as if forbidden from getting in.

The baby continues to cry.

He slides off the bed and goes to check the cot. Vulcan is there, yet he is turned on his stomach. As he moves his hand towards him, his son seems to get even further away. He opens his mouth to scream but it is as if his lips are melted into one another.

He puts more strength into his arm, yet the baby still seems to run away from him, sliding through space itself, together with the whole world.

He strains himself, feeling his veins about to pop in his temples. The crying intensifies. It blares right into his ear drums, still, it's not the ears that pain him as he tries to reach his son, but his heart as he is unable to soothe him.

He claws his fingers, as if trying to scratch into the fabric of space itself, to tear off the gap between them that seems to keep increasing. It is then that he feels it.

A warm pinprick.

It grows larger.

As it does, light gets sucked into it. The blinding whiteness of the outside spills in through the window. It swirls into his palm. Space itself distorts ever so slightly, just enough so his fingers bend and form the illusion of touch between him and his son.

He grasps onto his little shirt, the odd ball in his palm finally gone.

Vulcan is still crying. He wants to open his mouth to soothe him with some words, yet just like before, he simply cannot.

Instead, he spins the boy around, holding him on his back. It is then that his breathing stops; his heart, too, seems to fade away.

A grotesque stone mask adorns his son's face. It is large and pale and its features are contorted. The stoney lips, like two, thick, earthen worms start to stretch out past the boundaries of the mask.

The crying grows louder and Vulcan reaches out his small arms for his father. The space between them closes, and the hands grab at the sides of his head. He pulls his father close as the stone lips open wide, a dark, blind hole awaiting him as he gets swallowed up.

Sykes jumped back from the cot. His heart was racing and his whole body was covered in sweat.

Vulcan was asleep on his back, no trace of a mask on his face.

"Just a bad dream," he muttered to himself, turning his hand over and looking at his palm.

Out of sheer curiosity, he walked around the cot to look through the window into his back-garden. It was still night outside yet the moon started its descent towards the horizon. Somewhere in the distance, the red tinge of sunrise was starting to peek out.

He saw then, poking out from behind the chestnut tree, another mask.

"No," he muttered, quickly wiping his eyes, as if trying to brush away another dream. Yet once he opened them, the mask was still there.

It wasn't just the mask, either, but a whole person. Sykes couldn't tell whether it was a man or a woman. Whatever they were, they seemed to be occupied with something else entirely.

He pulled back from the window and stepped away from the cot. For a moment he considered what to do with Vulcan and decided on leaving him there to sleep. The safest place was in the house.

He hurried to the kitchen in search of a knife, dragging the kitchen-drawer slowly so as to not startle Vulcan and wake him.

With a weapon in hand, he paced towards the back door. As he opened it and stepped out into the night, he felt unsure of himself.

Montana always told me to get a gun for situations like these, he suddenly remembered, *now look at me.*

He crouched and moved slowly around the fence of his back garden, his presence guarded by shrubbery bushes. He made his way up behind the masked-figure, yet he was a good distance away. The knife was good for nothing.

He contemplated the distance between the two of them and wondered if he could make it to the tree before the figure had a chance of escaping.

No shot, Sykes shook his head, *you're no longer 20, old man.*

His heart was racing so much he could hear his pulse throbbing in his ears. He watched as the figure crouched. It had some sort of apparatus in its hand, running it over the ground as if checking for something.

Not 20, he reminded himself, *not 20 at all. Still,* something switched inside of him, *you're only 32.*

Right away he dashed out of the bushes. He didn't know what came over him. He had no intention of making use of the knife; he was no killer. He just wanted answers. The masks have appeared much too often in his life ever since he first saw those two in the parking lot at ICARUS.

For a good few steps, the figure suspected nothing. Sykes was completely silent. Yet as he got closer, the rustling of grass beneath his feet was loud enough for him to be able to overhear.

Yet it was too late.

"Come here!" Sykes growled, lurching himself forward, opening his arms as he prepared himself for impact.

"I'd rather not," the masked figure said, not even bothering to get to its feet or turn around. It simply raised its left hand above its head and clicked its fingers.

Sykes remained suspended in the air, unable to move.

"How far back do you want me to send you this time?"

This time?

"Should I rewind your memories as well, or should I spice it up?" the man chuckled, "leave you with them and see what you do. How's that? That sound good?"

What's he talking about?

"Wiping them doesn't seem to stop you from interfering. You've been at me the whole night," he shook his head, moving the device every ten seconds or so over the ground. It let out a crackle, lost and distorted. "If I tell you that I don't seek to harm you, will you believe me?"

His tone was harmless enough, yet still, he was a strange masked man in his back garden.

"I doubt it," he sighed, "but I mean it. I have no reason to harm a civilian. I easily could if I wanted to. You have no way to protect yourself against my power. I could send you back to your birth if I wanted to, you know?" he appeared to smile from his tone alone. "But I didn't. Of course, you wouldn't know that. But *I* know it."

What the hell is he going on about? Is this guy nuts?

"So I will do that for you, to see if anything changes. Good-bye now, and please, let me get on with my time."

His fingers clicked once more and the whole world spun backwards—all but for the masked man, it seemed.

Sykes found himself by the cot once more. His body ached just like before, yet his mind was no longer confused as to why.

The confusion came from somewhere else entirely—his memories.

He remembered it all. The knife, the sneaking, the masked man. Once more he worried that it might've been just a dream, so he stood up and went by the window.

The masked man was there, crouched, his little gadget hovering over the ground as he turned his head and looked directly at Sykes.

He gave him a friendly wave, pairing it together with a nod as he returned to his task.

"What the—"

Sykes bolted to the kitchen right away, picking up his knife. There was no point in sneaking anymore.

He dashed right out the back door and ran straight for him. Yet as he approached and clutched at the knife, something was out of place.

The masked man was not alarmed at all, as if Sykes was nothing but a harmless child.

"Knife again, really? the masked man asked. He stood up and turned to Sykes, watching him charge. "Third time tonight," he sighed. "I know you can't learn from erased memories, but come on. One would hope human nature would be less prone to violence."

And it was true. As Sykes closed in, he became more and more uncertain about his actions, all until his run slowed down to a jog, then to a walk, and then he found himself standing still, panting, eyes wide open, his hand shaking as he clutched the knife's hilt.

"What do you want from me?" he finally asked.

"Nothing, dammit! What don't you get? You're *irrelevant*. Just let me be and I'll be gone before you know it."

"And if I don't?"

"More trouble for my bosses. More trouble for my bosses means more trouble for me. More trouble for me...do I have to continue? Look, man, I agree. Time and place, right? Not great. But it wasn't anyone's choice. Not mine, not anyone's. But it has to be done quickly."

"*What* has to be done quickly?"

"Must I repeat myself? None of your business."

"I..."

"This must be confusing," the masked man nodded. Sykes tried to look at the design better. It was different from those two he saw in the parking lot, yet identical to the one he saw in his dream, placed over his son's face. "And to be frank, I won't explain it to you."

"You have to give me more reason to believe you won't want to harm me and my boy."

"Ah," the man nodded, "a child, then? That explains it. Family," he sighed, "of course. That makes more sense. See?" he pushed away from the tree, "I didn't even know this much about you, why would I seek to harm you?"

"I am trying to find the same thing out," Sykes shifted his grip on the knife.

"Listen," a groan escaped from behind the mask, "just let me finish this and I'll be on my way out," as he kneeled back down, "my work's cut out for me already. I didn't want him to crash land here. Nobody did, so—"

"Crash land?"

"Shit," the man spat, "there I am, spilling it all out. I might as well tell you his name, huh?" he cackled. "There must be a hole in my mouth, I just keep on spilling things. 'Suppose it's in my nature. It's too easy to get away with it when you can just, you know," he spun his finger in the air as if winding something back.

"Wait," Sykes stammered, "something...crashed here."

"Listen, it's none of your—"

"So it wasn't just a dream?"

The man suddenly stopped. His head snapped around and turned towards Sykes. He stood back up, slowly. He then took one step.

That is all. One step was enough and was right in front of him. Sykes' right hand felt tense and hot. The masked man let out a grunt.

"Don't look down," he said to Sykes, "I don't want you pan-icking."

Sykes did just that. His knife pierced through the man's body, his white suit starting to turn red around the chest.

"It's of no consequence to me," he sighed, "so don't worry about it. It's all fixable. Now," he cleared his throat, "tell me all that you know about this crash."

Sykes didn't understand. His whole body was shaking.

The clouds over the sky skipped positions unnaturally. The sun, too, was further up the horizon, as if it had sped us significantly for a moment before returning to normal.

Sykes could only look at the knife—at his hand holding it as he pierced the man's body.

"I *must* know," the man clutched Sykes' jaw and turned his head up, making him stare into his swirling stone eyes, "I *must* know all that you know about this crash. Do you understand?" his voice shook. "If I don't—*they...they will...*You don't even want to know, okay? Just...tell me."

Sykes wanted to speak, but his blood ran cold.

"I don't want to resort to threats. I am above that as a man," he spat, "don't make me sink to the level of a Non-Crafter."

Sykes shook his head.

"Fine. If it's the only language you people understand, then so be it. I will dirty my lips with it. Your *son*," he said, "exchange your information for his safety."

Something switched inside of Sykes at the mention of his son. His hand twitched as he stared at the mask.

All of a sudden, he could hear crying.

It was just like in that dream.

His free hand started to move up, slowly. The masked man paid no mind to it.

"Is that still not enough?!" the man growled. "I am not kidding! I have dirtied myself already, I can stoop lower! I can—"

The man stopped as Sykes pressed his clawed fingers against the centre of his chest—right next to the knife and the blood spilling out.

"What are you doing? I told you the wound is nothing, it—"

The same ball formed in Sykes' palm. It was black, yet its outlines glowed as it started to suck all of the light around it. Not only that, but the man's body began to distort, swirling like his masked eyes.

It all happened in an instant, really.

The man panicked, lifting his fingers in an attempt to click them, to rewind time and get himself away before it was too late.

"Fu—" was all that he managed to get out, his powers going to waste.

His body swirled into Sykes' palm, sucked up as if going down the drain, no trace of it left behind. No blood, no viscera, nothing. A clean erasure.

All the blood was on the knife and his other hand.

The blade then thudded onto the ground, followed by the odd scanning device.

Sykes remained still, staring at his palm, his hand still clawed and shaking.

CHAPTER SIX

He stood over the cot with the blade still in his hand. His hands shook, yet he couldn't get his eyes away from Vulcan, still sleeping peacefully.

I had to, he told himself, *for you, my boy. I...I never thought...but...*

He looked at his hands. He barely recognised them, yet they felt strong. Strong yet guilty.

He stood there a good while before he made it for the sink. The light of dawn leaked in through the windows, falling over his back. It was anything but warm.

The blood came off in trails, swirling into the drain hole. It was much too slow. He looked back over his shoulder, feeling some thick presence looming over him.

He tried to reach for the hilt so he could get it over quicker but his hand was still clawed. He didn't understand what he did.

He didn't understand at all.

It's for Vulcan's safety, he told himself, *whatever it was that I did, it was for **him**. **This blood,*** he talked himself through it all, *it means nothing. It can stain my hands, but it can't keep me from holding my boy.*

Sponge in hand, he started scrubbing at the knife

The clock said 6:43 once he was done and made it back to the cot. He checked on Vulcan, saw him asleep. He sat with his back to it, sliding into sleep on the stool

He woke up to the sound of his phone ringing. His body was stiff—frozen.

He picked it up: *Montana.*

"Shit," he checked the time; 7:55. "Yes, hello?"

"Were you asleep?"

"Sorta," he nodded, twisting himself to look into the cot. Vulcan was awake but quiet, just looking up at the ceiling. "Good boy," he whispered, bringing his hand forward to tickle his tummy. He stopped himself short; blood stained his fingers. "Fuck."

"Are you listening to me, Sykes?" Montana asked petulantly.

"What? Yes," he squeezed the phone between his jaw and shoulder to look at his other hand. Blood on it, too—a lot less, though. "I think, actually. No, sorry. I just woke up. Can you say that again?" he got up, "just two seconds," he whispered to his boy as he left for the kitchen.

"I'll be there in 5."

"What? Why in 5? Pick him up after work; that's what we said."

"Can't do. Going somewhere with Dylan."

"Dylan?" Sykes found himself mouthing. He reached the sink, got the tap running with hot water as he put his hands under it. "Who's Dylan?"

"Don't do this to me," she said. He could feel the roll of her eyes in her voice.

"Alright, then—what will you do with him?"

"With who, with Dylan?" she sounded baffled, "what the hell are you asking, Sykes, are you out of your mind?"

"With Vulcan, you lunatic," he sighed, "what will you do with Vulcan after work?"

"Oh…right, yeah. Well, we're taking him with us. We're going camping for the weekend."

"Camping; great."

"So 5 minutes, yes?"

"Eh..." he scrubbed and scrubbed at his fingers, the red stain not coming off. *I really did kill him, huh? It wasn't just a dream.* "Sure, yeah."

"You don't sound sure."

"Well I don't have *shit* ready, Montana, of course I'm not sure. I just woke up. I didn't expect this."

"It's fine, I'll help. You sound on edge; are you alright, by the way?"

"What, yes, I'm good. Just bad sleep," he looked at his hands, "shit. Yeah, just bad sleep."

"Just sleep in after," she said.

"Can't. Got work."

"Work?" she sounded surprised. "You found work?"

Fuck.

"Where?" she continued.

"Uhm, well, you know. Just some coffee shop downtown."

"Oh come on, Sykes, you're not in college anymore."

"It's better than having nothing at all, is it not?"

She said nothing. The silence allowed him to move. He turned off the tap.

"I'm pulling up right now," she chose not to push further.

"Okay. Bye."

"Wh-"

He cut her off, threw the phone aside and rushed back in his room.

If she sees me with blood on my hands, it's all going to shit.

He popped open a cabinet and stuck on the first pair of gloves; leather, black, clean, no sign of wear whatsoever.

The car engine hummed outside.

"Already?"

Vulcan must've felt the presence of his mother for he stood on his feet in his cot.

"Mama, mama!" he waved his hands.

"Yes, yes, mama is here."

"Sykes," the door pushed open, "I'm here, come on."

"You left your car running—and hey, don't just come into my—"

"You look like shit," she sighed looking at him, "what's with the gloves?"

"What?"

"The gloves," she pointed at them as she swiftly moved towards Vulcan's cot, "hey baby boy, how are you doing?"

"Mama-mama!"

She picked him up and carried him with one arm, giving him a kiss on his cheek.

"You're gonna answer me or what?"

"Bad circulation," he shrugged.

"Come on…you can do better than that."

They looked at one another, but as soon as Montana saw that he had nothing to say for himself, she gave up on it.

"It's alright. Nappies and toys—where do you keep them?"

"Oh, right."

He turned and moved to the left, opening a large drawer.

"How many do you need?"

"As much, I ran out," she said, "we could stop to get some on the way, though. Yeah, we'll do that, just give me—"

"Have these," he took out a whole pack, "I have plenty left. It's probably out of the way for you. Did you take time off work?" he asked.

"No, Sykes. I told you we're going right after—Dylan and I."

"Who's Dylan?" he asked, deeply confused.

"You need sleep. You're wired."

"I—"

"Where are his toys?"

"Which ones?"

"Well, the ones you have—where's that plushy cat he likes, the soft one."

"Hold on," he leaves the room to look around. He finds it somewhere in the bathroom. "Here," he handed it to her. "Anything else? I assume you'll get him ready for camping; you don't need anything more from me?"

"You got any thick socks for him by any chance?" she asked.

He went to have a look. One drawer, then another. "No."

"Are you sure you're alright?"

"Yes, why?"

"You're shaking all over. You're pale. You can tell me, you know. I'm not some monster."

He stood up and looked at her. He saw for a moment—for the first time in a long while—the woman he fell in love with some time back. He saw her so well he almost spilled it all out.

Luckily, her phone rang.

She slid Vulcan from one shoulder to the other, lifting her knee as she took out her phone from her pocket.

"Yes, babe?"

Babe? Sykes cringed, *she used to hate that.*

"I'm picking him up right now. Yes," she nodded, taking a look at Sykes. She shook her head. *Pity?* He wondered, *God, what the fuck. Why pity?* "Bye," she mouthed soundlessly.

"What about—" he whispered as he pointed at the nappies and toy.

"Sure."

He picked them up and carried them to her car.

"Hand him over," he said, resting the items atop the car. "And pop the door, will you?" and as soon as she did he placed Vulcan in his chair, strapping him up as Montana got behind the wheel.

"The trunk?" he asked and she popped it. He carried the items and arranged them neatly in there, all rather quickly.

He made it to her window, watching her still taking the call.

"Thanks," she whispered, putting the car into gear.

Sykes didn't move.

"I said thanks, Sykes. What's the matter?"

"Finish the call," he nodded. "You're not doing that—not with Vulcan in the back."

"Oh, come on."

Sykes shook his head. His gloved hand caught onto the rim of the window frame and squeezed. The leather groaned.

"Just finish it."

"Listen, Dylan, we'll talk when I get home, Sykes won't let me leave. No," she sighed, "it's not *serious* like that. He's just being silly. He's tired or something. He works as a barista now," she said, mockingly, "must be *exhausting*. Okay, love you babe, bye. Happy?" she threw the phone onto the passenger seat.

"All good," he pulled back.

She rolled up the window and drove off without a word. He watched them go, his hands cold.

As soon as they were out of sight, he went back inside, checked the time again—8:13—and threw himself in bed, falling right asleep.

He woke up way too late. There were some missed calls from Clara on his phone and as soon as he got to his feet, he called in sick.

No questions were asked whatsoever. Perhaps his voice communicated all that was needed. The day was simple and long.

I need to get some things in order. He went into the kitchen and picked up the clean knife. He then took an apple and stepped out into his backyard, right by the spot where it all had happened.

There, in the grass, the stone device remained. He sat down, crossing his legs as he started slicing the apple

Slice 1

*I killed a man. Well, I am **pretty sure** I did. I did it out of anger. I felt nothing the instant it happened. That instant, though, seemed to extend on forever.*

Slice 2

*I killed a man to protect Vulcan. The anger was my fight or flight response. I **had** to do it. There was no other choice. I remember feeling guilt, but it was brief. What I felt most was relief. My boy is safe.*

Slice 3

*Is it okay to move over this so quickly? I should feel worse. I **killed** someone. No matter the reason, why...why don't I feel the weight*

of it as much as I should? I'm not some nutjob, am I? How did I even kill him?

Slice 4

*I am a Crafter. I am certain now. Whatever came out of my hand—both in my dream and in action—was an ability. I was much too angry to remember how it felt to put my powers into action. If I were to go by Ms. Clothos' explanation, it doesn't make sense. I haven't lied to myself about any rules of the world. I didn't bend anything. I was just angry. She must be lying. But then again, the original concept of an **epiphany** didn't come by me either. I hadn't uncovered anything...and yet...I killed a man with an ability.*

Slice 5

*Who the hell was that? That's the third masked figure. Will they all come here? Is Vulcan **not** safe? They must know I killed him. It's good that he is with his mother. I need to bring this to someone—to the police? No...all they would have is my blood and no body. I would be in trouble. Icarus? No, I would seem suspicious. Gilbert? Most definitely...he could work.*

Slice 6

There really was a man that crashed here. It wasn't a dream. He did something to me, but I can't remember what. I can't remember what he said, either. But that's a question for another time.

Slice 7

The masked people know me. There's more, they'll come back. I haven't a clue about my powers. I need to get my shit together.

Apple finished.

The whole time, the stone was right before him. He did not touch it.

He inspected the knife and then stabbed it into the ground. He stuck out his hand, taking off his glove as he clawed his fingers again, trying to emulate the power from before.

Nothing came.

"Come on," he groaned, "dammit."

Multiple futile attempts got him sweaty with strain and to his feet. Nothing came out for hours. Not a single spark.

"Sykes?" a frail, old voice trailed through the air.

"Sorry?" he looked up. "Oh," he smiled, looking over the fence at a small, old lady, her hair white and tied up in a messy bun. "Mrs. Dolloray, how are you doing?"

"You look a little frightened, dear," she said. "Are you alright?"

"Just fine," he smiled.

"But your clothes are all creased up," she shook her head, "should I come over and iron them for you?"

"Please, Mrs. Dolloray..."

"It's just been so long since I've been in your mother's home," she sighed, "I just..."

Sykes let his arms drop at his side. "I'm sorry, Mrs. Dolloray. But I can't, not right now."

"The little man's asleep?"

"No-no," he shook his head and groaned, "he's gone camping with his mother for the weekend," as he leaned down and picked up the device.

"Oh, Montana. How is she? Faring well?"

"What, yeah, I suppose. We don't talk much."

"That's a pity," she hissed. "It's a pity for the boy, really. Since she left you, I can tell that your family just hasn't been—"

His heart started to flare up, an intense heat spreading over his chest. His teeth gritted against his will and he tried to swallow his words as he looked at the old woman.

Yet as he was reaching his wits, a *beep* took his attention.

It came from his hand.

He lifted the device to his face and saw that the swirls had turned blue.

"...there's nothing wrong with getting some help, I mean..."

He lifted it closer to his face.

What's going on?

"...that poor baby boy, to have his parents in such a situation. How is he going to grow? Do you never think of that?..."

This got activated just now—how? Why?

He found a blue light falling like a curtain over the ground, sparse swirls, invisible to the eye, appearing beneath it. As he moved around his garden, the device crackled, revealing some more swirls here and there.

"Are you listening to me, Sykes?"

"Mhmm...yeah."

What was he scanning? What are these traces?

He paced around some more but couldn't figure out a damn thing.

"...just think of poor Vulcan and—"

"Mrs. Dolloray, I must get inside," he cut her short.

"Already?

"Places to be," he smiled, or tried to, at least. He wasn't sure if it came out alright, but Mrs. Dolloray of all people wasn't going to question him. "Look at me, you said it yourself. These clothes are a mess. I got to change."

"You need help wi—"

"No, no, I'm good."

"Would you tell Montana to stop by my place when she comes to drop off your boy?"

"Sure," he turned and paced towards his house.

He waited outside of the bar. It was 6:05 and no one was there. He put his hand in his pocket and found the device. He fingered it slightly but did not take it out.

The sky was starting to darken and as he held his fingers to the stone, so did his thoughts. Amongst those worries, though, one thought alone seemed to rise deep out of his subconscious and as it formed his heart seemed to race with joy.

Each time, it popped before it fully got to the forefront of his mind.

"It can't be that," he shook his head.

He patted himself down until he found an old pack of smokes.

"I haven't worn this jacket in ages."

He looked at the packet, not even opened.

"I didn't know you smoked, Mr. St. Jane," Clara's voice appeared out of nowhere.

"Oh, hi," he smiled, "I don't," he put the packet back. "I quit a while ago—when Vulcan was born."

"Good. Still having thoughts about it?"

"It's the smokes you quit, not the cravings," he shrugged. "Where's everyone else?"

"It's a habit to run late. Come," she walked past him. She wore black pumps paired with a burgundy, silk dress pants and burgundy, silk dress shirt. She had a nice, golden watch on her left wrist and a necklace just as golden wrapped around her neck. "Let's go in."

The sign said *The Underworld*. It was neon, but not turned on; it wasn't dark enough.

Clara led the way and Sykes—as much as he wanted to—couldn't advert his gaze from her figure. The clothes she wore at work did not favour her body as much as the ones she was wearing at that moment.

"What's with the get-up?"

"Are you checking me out?" she purred, not turning her head.

"I'd get in trouble for that."

"Right," she chuckled. "You don't like it?"

"I'm just asking. It's so...business-like."

"It's a little more casual than work. Here," she nodded to a waiter that seated us down at a large booth. The bar had a live jazz band playing, not too loudly, just enough to mellow the body down. "What about you? Not keen on fashion" she chuckled.

"Huh?" He sat right across from her, watching her put her handbag down at her side. It was black and he didn't notice it until then.

"Come on," she tapped her long nails against the wooden table, "you can't be serious. You're wearing the *exact* same clothes."

"So?"

"What do you mean *so*," she scoffed. "You're out in the world, let yourself *be* a little."

"You see," he leaned his elbow against the backrest of his seat, "that's the difference between people like me and people like you, Clara. I let myself *be* all the time."

"Ha-ha!" she rolled her eyes, "right."

"*This* is me, at work, here, at home. I'm always just who I am. No need for fronts," he shrugged.

"Mr. St. Jane," she feigned offence, "are you calling me two-faced?"

"You caught me," he put his arms up in the air, drawing a chuckle out of her.

She reached into her purse and took out some lipstick and a pocket mirror. She looked at herself, reapplying it.

"Nice place, no?" she asked, briefly glancing at him.

"Hmm? Yeah, sure," he nodded.

Silence fell over them again. He was thankful for the jazz band otherwise he would have disappeared into his seat with awkwardness. There was a clear divide between them that he could not see—only feel.

They were sitting in a smoking area. Sykes got twitchy, looking around. Plums of smoke rose from other booths.

"The others coming any time soon?"

Time was 6:25.

"You don't like my company?" she asked. The waiter came just then. "A martini for me," she ordered.

"And you, sir?"

"A G&T."

"Any specific gin?"

"Beefeater?" he looked towards Clara. She shrugged, as if telling him, *your choice.*

The waiter looked at him funny, nodded, and left.

"What was that all about?"

"Eh," she waved her hand in front of her face, "don't mind him."

"No-no-no. I need to know. *That*," Sykes leaned over, drawing so close that she couldn't help but feel like she was getting in on a secret, so she drew in, too, a childish smile on her face, "That was personal. I *need* to know."

"The gin's just cheap," she chuckled. "It's nothing serious."

"Gin is gin," he shrugged. "What, did he want me to break the piggy-bank?"

Clara mimicked slamming a hammer down. "More tips for him, maybe?"

"Yeah, right," he chortled. "As if we're not going to leave him a fat tip after."

"Oh boy," she shook her head, "just you wait. Here," she grabbed her bag, "you don't mind if I smoke, do you?

"You smoke?"

"On special occasions."

"That's what they all say," he chuckled.

"*They* who?"

"Addict smokers. You catch them at any moment of the day and that—that *smell* is about them. *Special occasions* my ass."

"Hey," she pouted, ready to defend herself. "Being *alive* is a special enough thing, isn't it? A woman's allowed to have her smoke."

"Well...if you put it that way, then be my guest," he smiled.

"Thank you," she returned the favour.

He watched her light up her smoke. She took a long drag, narrowing her eyes, letting the smoke wash up her face.

"It really *is* the worst gin out there," she chuckled, looking through the curtain of smoke right into his eyes. "

"Come on," he rolled his eyes, "it makes no difference."

"What makes no difference?" a loud voice echoed from behind them.

Sykes didn't turn.

"Diego," Clara nodded, lifting her cigarette. "Want one?"

"Pass it over, *chiquita*," he cackled. "Who's this?"

"Sykes St. Jane," Sykes stood up, extending his hand. "The Muffin Man."

Diego looked Sykes up and down. "So formal," he cackled, clasping his hand, "but no suit."

"He hates suits."

"Do you now?" Diego smiled, "cool. Give me one, Clara."

"Will you ever buy your own?" she asked.

"When it'll be worth it. I don't smoke that often. Scoot over," he waved her up the seat, sitting next to her. He wore a red Hawaiian shirt with a pair of black shorts and black vans. He had a silver earring in his left earlobe and one of his incisors was golden.

"Neither do I, but I still have my own pack. You're a deadbeat."

"Hey, come on now," he scowled, "don't paint a bad image for our new friend over here—uh—Say—"

"Sykes."

"Sykes, right," he tapped the table. "Here, listen, Sykes. Just wanted you to know that you replaced one guy that was very dear to us. Big shoes to fill—no pressure, though."

"Sure," he chuckled.

"What are you guys drinking?" Diego asked

"Martini for me and for hi—ah," Clara smiled, "the waiter's here."

Diego turned to the waiter, inspected the glasses. "Who got a Beefeater?"

"I did," Sykes raised his hand.

"Christ, man. Here, take that back," he picked it up the moment the waiter put it on the table and placed it back on the tray.

"Sir…"

"Diego, it's okay—"

"No it's not okay, Christ. Beefeater?" he rolled his eyes. "Here, you guys still have Plymouth?"

The waiter nodded. "Get him some of that. Sprinkle some wildflower in there, too, will you?"

Sykes gritted his teeth as he watched the waiter go.

"There was no need for that," he said.

"Ease up," Diego chuckled and looked at Clara, "he always this tense?"

Clara shrugged.

"That smoke you owe me?"

"I don't owe you anything," she smiled and passed him one either way and then the lighter. He lit up, leaned back and extended his arm over the backrest, going past Clara's shoulder.

Sykes eyed the motion curiously. Clara didn't wince away. She sipped her martini and then smiled at Sykes.

"What's wrong?"

"Nothing. I'm just wondering where all the others are."

"There something wrong with us?" Diego asked, jokingly.

Sykes just lifted his hands placatingly.

"What's your deal?" Diego puffed his way.

"My deal?"

"You don't drink—clearly, the Beefeater, Christ—you don't smoke. What do you do? Free time, I mean."

"I spend time with my child."

Diego's eyes widened. He looked at Clara and she gave him a smile right back. "He's not lying. He has a 2 year old boy. I don't blame him, he's a cutie."

"Christ," he cackled, "so you're a family man, eh? Then sorry for getting you that drink, starting you off early? Suppose your missus will mind if you come home shitfaced?"

"I don't live with my wife anymore. We're separated."

"Are ya now?" Diego smiled, leaning over, "she looking for someone?"

"Diego!" Clara smacked him across the back of the head.

"Alright, alright I was just joking."

He leaned back and dragged some more from his smoke. In due time Sykes drink came to him and he let it sit there on the table before him as he looked around. He didn't know how to warm up to Diego but for the time being he didn't care for it. He just wanted the others to come.

They spilled in one after the other shortly after he took his first sip of drink. It was as if it sped up the whole process and as he stood up and greeted them one by one he could feel Clara's eyes on him.

Gilbert and Cole came together and sat right next to Sykes. Gilbert didn't bother changing out of his work clothes and Cole just had a black button-down shirt that was different, otherwise, it was just office attire.

"We drinking?"

"I'm not," Cole piped up.

"Yeah yeah. Look at you, Sykes, got a drink before you, thought you had a little one to take care of."

"Wife's out camping with him over the weekend."

"Hear that?" Gilbert leaned back and threw a look Diego's way, "get him proper drunk, *ese.*"

"Don't say that to me I'll restructure your jaw," Diego cackled.

"Christ someone get some drinks into him too before he actually does it," Gilbert shook his head. "Over here," he called the waiter, "three vodka shots for me. You, Cole?"

"Evian water."

"Evian?" Gilbert questioned, "why Evian?"

"It's so sweet," Clara sighed.

Diego seemed to agree, too. Sykes was completely lost. Luckily for him a face he recognised appeared. Kashmere had on a white dress that opened up above the knees, red and pink and orange flowers embroidered into hems of it and around the chest. She paired them with a pair of open white heels and a red bracelet around her left ankle.

"Hey everyone, sorry I'm late," she excused herself and sat down.

"Don't worry about it," Clara told her and the whole topic of being late had disappeared into nothingness as she ordered a martini for herself.

Sykes sipped cautiously at his own drink and he found himself with half the glass emptied when Diego and Clara and ordered another round and Gilbert got himself 3 more shots.

Cole got another water.

"You not liking it?" Clara lit herself another cigarette. Her whole face was covered in smoke as they spoke he could barely see her.

Sykes shrugged. "It's alcohol. It's all the same to me."

"As if," Gilbert rolled his eyes, "is something wrong with your tongue?"

"You leave him alone," Clara snapped.

"Oop," Diego looked surprised, "you warmed up to our new Muffin Man real quick, Clara."

"It's cause I'm more involved!"

"Ha! Is that what they call it nowadays?" Gilbert slicked his hair back to get it out of his eyes.

"Why, you—""It's true, though," Cole defended her, "she was the same with Grigory, wasn't she?"

"She's just a vixen this one," Diego wrapped his hand around her and pulled her close, giving her a kiss on the cheek. Clara flushed and something turned inside of Sykes, "she's all over these new rookies."

"May I ask, you know—*what* happened?" Sykes looked around, yet judging by the look on their faces, he quickly realised that he *may* not.

"Nothing really," Gilbert groaned after enough silence. "Just wasn't cut out to be a Crafter—agh! Sure, yeah," he nodded, rubbing his shin where Kashmere kicked him, "I deserve that one."

"He died in combat?" Sykes was mesmerised, "as a Muffin Man?"

Gilbert shrugged. "You might be next," he passed him a knowing glance, one that only the two of them understood, yet the others tried to take as a joke. "With all this new chaos unleashed by that interview...sheesh," he sighed. "Non-Crafters might come after our necks."

"D'you guys see that 10 year old Crafter out of Japan?" Diego added, trying to move the unwanted subject along, "here, pass another smoke," he tapped Clara on the shoulder, whispering to her. She cheered up a little at his voice and passed him one, "they'll have to change the laws to do something about these underage Crafters."

"Why?" Sykes wondered. "It's a great thing, being a Crafter.

"Yeah, being a good one," Diego said.

"Exactly," Gilbert pointed at his friend, as if to pick up where he left off. "The more we multiply, the harder it is to keep the Crafters under control. Right now, most States' powers are stretched thin with the scarce few numbers that we have. It's been a problem for a while, that's why we got these companies and agencies, like ICARUS, just sorta...helping. That's all good," he stopped for a moment as he got hold of the waiter, "where are my three shots that I ordered? Yeah, please, my throat is dry." He waited for the waiter to go and then returned. "Thing is, with the pace we're multiplying at—maybe not so much here in America, but like, worldwide, and really, this is a problem concerning the whole world, so you can't just be blind to it."

"Not at all," Diego added in, tipping what was left of his drink down his throat. As the waiter returned with the three shots for Gilbert, Diego signalled for yet another Martini.

"Smart water for me," Gilbert said, "and two more shots."

"What Gilbert is trying to say," Kashmere leaned forward, "in *fewer* words, is that more nutcase Crafters are popping up, unauthorised ones. They don't help with our image at all and by God do we need to clean it up lately."

"It's happening much faster than the agencies and states can keep up with," Clara puffed the words out together with the smoke. "So we're spread just as thin. We make due with all we have."

Diego groaned again. His foot tapped restlessly. "The thing with Grigory," he croaked and the room grew heavy, "he was needed, *chico*," the boisterous man from before seemed to peel away, leaving space for a mourning, reserved individual. "Duty called and Gilbert answered. Sadly," he shrugged, "he didn't hold the line the whole way through. It got cut short. Must've run out of credit," he shrugged, "aaah!"

"You idiot!" Clara slapped him again.

"Come on, I'm just easing the mood. Look at him," he pointed at Sykes, "he's on edge, about to lose his mind."

"You won't die in battle as a Muffin Man," Cole nudged him, trying to sound reassuring. He sounded nothing of the sort.

"Icarus changed some rules around that. Even if you're the last man standing you wouldn't be called."

"Last man standing?" he looked confused, "but I thought—you guys *lose*?" "Sheesh," Gilbert shook his head, "I've missed out on *too* many funerals, buddy."

"You're all so insensitive," Kashmere hissed. "Waiter!" she called.

"Cut us some slack. We're just hardened by battle. But we're nothing like those U6s."

"U6s?"

"Upper Echelon," Gilbert tapped his knuckles on the table. "Hey, is anyone else supposed to come?"

"Terry was meant to be here. Cianna, too."

"You called Cianna?" Gilbert sounded surprised.

"Yeah, why not?"

Gilbert simply shrugged.

"Terry never shows up to these meetings anymore," Cole sounded depressed.

"He doesn't hang around with our kind anymore," Kashmere shrugged, "a *Sex on the Beach* please?" she nodded to the waiter, "he's management now."

"Yeah, whatever," Gilbert rolled his eyes.

"Envious much?"

"Ack—" he threw his hand her way. "You look like you need another drink, Sykes."

He shook his head. "I didn't even finish this one."

"Then finish it and get another one. I told you, you look like you need one."

"Ah—"he waved his hand, "no, no."

"Waiter—another uhm...whatever it is that he was having. But make it a little weaker so he actually drinks it."

The waiter nodded, left, and was sure to return.

"Finish that one before he comes with the next or you're finished," Gilbert warned him and Sykes didn't know whether jokingly or not.

Either way, he grabbed the drink and chugged it down.

"See? Now that's what I'm talking about. Now," he cleared his throat, "why won't you tell us, Sykes, what is it you specialise in?"

"Huh?"

"Your Craft...your grade, your degree, come on, man," Diego snapped his fingers, "you ain't slow are you? Not that there's anything wrong with that, but you've got to tell us so we know how to treat you."

"I'm not slow."

"Thank fuck," Diego leaned back, relieved.

Sykes tried to look to Clara for comfort and all he got was a smile.

"He doesn't know," she answered for him.

"What?" Cole looked at him.

"Yeah, *what* is right?"

"Guys," Sykes put his hands on his head.

"Is that drink hitting you? Just one drink?"

"I'm light-weight," he shook his head.

He was a little tipsy, feeling his words slipping from his tongue.

"Okay but what do you mean you don't know what you specialise in?"

Sykes shrugged. "I don't know. I never had an epiphany."

"Like fuck you didn't," Diego slammed his palm on the table. "This guy is a jester! He's joking us, isn't he? Who does he think he is?"

"Would you calm down?" Clara tapped his chest, "he's not joking. I was the one that checked him, for what—like 2 whole years? He never made it past the scan. Then one day...he did."

"The whole scanner system went up in flames," Kashmere smiled.

"That was *you*?" Diego pointed at him, "what, are you like crazy strong or something?"

"Listen to yourself, he would've been much more than a Muffin Man if that were the case."

"I guess," Diego shrugged, looking around. "What if he's like Cianna?"

"Oh, please," Clara rolled her eyes. "She's the only one that does it and it's for security reasons."

"Does what?" Sykes asked.

"Eh," Clara shrugged. "She hides her Craft. No one really knows what she does."

"Or *if* she does anything at all," Diego cackled. Clara turned and glared at him. "What?"

"Just watch that mouth of yours before you get in trouble."

"Cut him some slack," Gilbert smiled, "it's what we're all thinking, isn't it?" he shrugged, "we're out there fighting—even the likes of me—and she never shows up. What can a guy do but question?"

"Your conspiracy theories are just *that*," she pointed a half-smoked cigarette at them in turn. "She's most likely just privileged that she's the Director's sister."

"That's bad enough for me," Gilbert said.

"Well, nobody asked you."

"We're having a damn conversation," he mumbled.

"Hey, guys," Kashmere pushed forward some snacks, "just munch on these and calm down, alright?"

"Sweet," Gilbert reached for some nuts.

Diego's eyes didn't leave Sykes the entire time. "Come on, *chico*. Don't be secretive. Will you tell us?"

"I don't have anything to tell you," he said, "honest to God. I didn't have an epiphany."

"Bull-shit!"

"Come on, Diego. You said it yourself—the world is weird, right? The rules are ever changing. Nobody knows what's going on."

"Yes but this *guy* didn't have shit. You can't *not* have shit and be a Crafter."

"Guys, please..."

Sykes was lucky that the waiter returned. He didn't know what came over him but as soon as he got his hands on his drink he downed the whole lot, needing a little bit more courage.

They looked at him but said nothing.

"I mean it, alright?" Sykes wiped his mouth. "One day I was nothing and now I am here."

"Well, can you...can you materialise anything?"

Sykes felt his hand clawing over his knee. His leg was shaking and he could feel something coming out. Remembering what happened last time that it did, he stood himself up with a burst.

"Easy now."

"I just need to get to the toilet," he said.

"Need help?" Clara asked.

"Yeah Clara, go help him hold his dick," Diego cackled, "be serious. We'll be here, Muffin Man, don't worry."

Awkwardly he waddled to the toilet, getting himself in a stall as he sat down, looking at his hands.

"What's going on?"

The world was shaking in front of his eyes and his heart would not rest.

CHAPTER SEVEN

A black BMW pulled up in front of the house. Two masked figures stepped out; a man and a woman.

The woman checked her watch, stretching out her arm and revealing the end of a golden-etched tattoo on her wrist.

"Come on," she said, "I got to be somewhere."

"Is that all you do, rush people?" the man asked. He took a stone device out of his pocket.

"What are you doing with that?" she stepped up and took it from his hands. "There's no need. We know the stone's here."

"I just wanted to make sure," he muttered.

"Stop making sure and make yourself useful instead," she hissed. "That idiot, Time, already failed. We screw this up—

"Tsk. I get it!"

The man looked over his shoulder. He was skittish. The woman stood tall, confident; in a hurry.

"Did you check if—"

"Yes, yes," she nodded, looking at her watch again. "You did it well. Everyone's asleep."

"Alright," his mechanical voice crackled. "Just so you know, I'll put in a complaint," he said, crouching down on the pavement, bringing his right palm towards the lawn connecting to the house in front of them. "You promised me independence."

"Total independence does not exist. You are given what *most* people get. Is that really a complaint?"

"Yes!"

"Listen to me, Arthur. If we can't help them find where that fool of a man disappeared off to, independence will be the least of your concerns, you understand?"

"Yes, Cybress..."

"Then shut up and transport the damn evidence!"

The man shook his head. The skin on his hand peeled back, revealing an intricate machine skeleton underneath. A barrel—like that of a shotgun—found itself in the centre of each of his palms. He pressed them onto the ground and *pushed*, pulses of energy emanating from his body.

The woman looked on as invisible waves spread over the lawn. Under their weight, the very structure of the ground and everything they touched lost its hardness, undulating after his will, as if made out of rubber.

Once more she checked her watch. The tip of her foot tapped impatiently against the pavement. Restless, she started pacing back and forth behind the hunched man.

The waves quickly expanded, reaching the house. Its integrity was compromised as it started to bend and wobble.

"Make sure not to break anything," she said, "we need everything intact for the analysis."

"Yeah, yeah, I get it."

A harsh, white light poked through the tin holes that formed the eyes of the stone mask.

"Are you done?"

The man only growled as the rubber-bendy house started to pull towards his palm like strands of spaghetti undulating, getting whisked away until nothing was left but the empty lawn with a chestnut tree at the back.

"Now I am," he stood up, pulling the flaps of skin back over his palm, "it's all stored."

Without a word the woman stepped back into the car.

"Let's go," she said, pulling down the window, "it's done, Arthur. We've got to split."

"I can just—"

She shook her head. "You got to drive me there."

"Can't you just get a cab?"

"I got to change, you idiot. You want me to change in some stranger's cab?"

Arthur mumbled something under his breath as he made his way around the car, got in, and drove off.

"A little faster," she said, starting to take off her clothes.

Arthur stepped on the gas.

A fist thumped on the stall door.

"Hey, Muffin Man, are you still in there, buddy?" Diego's voice echoed through the toilet.

Sykes seemed to awake from his stupor. He had stared at his clawed hand so much that now it was as if the imprint of it was etched into the fabric of reality.

He stood up, wobbly, but not completely drunk.

"I'm here, yeah," he said.

"You alright?"

"Y-yeah," he unlocked the stall and opened the door. Diego was much taller and wider when he stood in front of him. There was an endearingly soft look on his face. *Is it pity?* Sykes wondered. "I'm good."

By instinct he stepped towards the sink to wash his hands, although he didn't do anything but stare at it in the stall.

As the cold water ran over his fingers the colour seeped out of his flesh and spilled into the white sink.

"Have you killed, Diego?" Sykes asked, his voice as distant as his gaze.

"Killed?"

Sykes nodded. "In action, I mean."

"Yes, of course. Many times." He seemed to say it with pride.

"How do you get over it?"

"What's there to get over?" he shrugged. "The people I killed had no respect for everyone else's lives, why would I have any for theirs?"

"I...I don't know."

"It's not that deep," Diego stepped forward, leaning over the sink next to Sykes. He was looking at him through the mirror. Their eyes met, but the reflection formed a bridge between their gazes that seemed to lengthen with each passing second, getting them further away from one another. "Unless you make it deep."

"And - and what if you do?"

"Then you're fucked. You'll be left with guilt so bad you can't wash your own ass, man. That's no good. As a Crafter, one must *act* according to their values first. If your values are so weak that some bloodshed pisses all over them," he shrugged, "then you aren't up for it. Why are you asking me all this, anyway?" Diego clamped his hand so suddenly on his shoulder that Sykes jolted, "did you get your hands dirty, Muffin Man?"

"Wh-what? N-no."

Diego paused for a moment.

"Then? What's the problem?"

"I'm just thinking, that's all."

"That whole talk with Gregory got in your head, didn't it?" he drew close. "It's alright, come on, splash some cold water on your face and let's get back. We shouldn't have mentioned it—our bad, alright? But don't worry. You'll be safe. There won't be any blood on your hands as long as you're a Muffin Man, and neither will your life be at risk. We've got it all covered, cool?"

"Cool, yeah," Sykes washed and washed and washed away the colour from his hands, a red only he could see spilling down the drain.

He did as he was told, splashing water on his face and when he lifted his head his face was covered in blood. He wanted to scream but held it in.

"Good, let's get back then."

Diego squeezed his shoulder once more and led the way back to the booth.

"Hey, hey, hey! I brought him back from the dead!"

"Oh, come on, it wasn't that serious," Sykes excused himself, looking for the waiter. As he sat down, he raised his hand, seeing him, called him over, "a water, any kind, doesn't matter," and ordered.

"Good good, stick on the water," Diego sat down next to Clara.

"You okay, Mr. St. Jane—for sure?" she asked.

"Yes," he nodded. "Who's that?" he whispered, nodding towards the corner of the booth. Somebody new was sitting down. An elegant, gorgeous woman with long, ginger hair. She had on a black shoulderless dress and from her left shoulder, a golden dragon wrapped itself down her arm, all the way to her wrist.

Wait— his head began to buzz.

"The chick with the tattoo? That's the big boss' assistant, but more importantly, his sister." Diego said, "hey, Cianna," he shouted over the table. "Sykes over here wants to know who you are?"

Cianna was in the middle of talking to Kashmere, deep into some topic. She turned her head—only slightly—to look at him. Green, piercing eyes. Crimson lips—pearly white teeth.

As she looked at him, her gaze seemed to coil with his.

It can't be—can it? The noise in his head crackled like static. It got so loud he could barely hear the others.

"Is there...something we must know?" Diego cleared his throat. You two got around to one another before?" he winked at Sykes.

"What? No, God—Jesus..." Sykes' reaction was delayed. His words, once they came out of his mouth, didn't sound like they belonged to him.

"Oh, come on, Sykes," Cianna bashfully winked at him. "There's no need to hide, is there?"

"Oho?" Clara's brows raised in tandem as she turned to Sykes. "What's this? Spill out *all* the secrets!"

"There are *no* secrets, I swear!" Sykes waved his hands placatingly.

"Big dog sleeps with the Director's sister," Gilbert shook his head, "by God."

"Hey, hey!" Cianna intervened, pointing an accusatory finger at Gilbert, "now don't you take it there, alright? Contrary to popular belief, I don't sleep around with anyone I get my hands on."

"Hear that?" Gilbert turned to Sykes, "you're just *anyone* buddy."

"Guess that settles that," Diego deflated, leaning back. "The rumour was good while it lasted, Sykes. For a brief moment, you shone like a Golden God to me."

"See who I have to work with?" Cianna turned to Sykes. "My brother *relies* on these people. Can you believe that?"

Sykes shook his head.

"You know," she laced her fingers onto the table, "I feel like there's some discriminatory undertones here."

"By God," Gilbert hissed, "I need another 3 or 4 shots if you start with that again."

"No-no," she wiggled her finger. "Just because I'm ginger, what—my soul is tainted?"

"You said it," Gilbert shrugged.

"Mhmm," she narrowed her eyes at him. "So if I sleep with everyone, how come I haven't gotten to you yet, Gilbert? I wonder."

"Yeesh," Diego made a cutting motion over his own throat. "That's a wrap, folks. Change subjects."

"Was never interested," Gilbert said.

Cianna cackled. "I love this," she took a sip out of her drink through straw. "Let me know when you're interested, alright? Maybe we can fix something up to make you less envious."

"Will let you know, love."

"Thanks," she smiled, turning back to Sykes. "Look," she pointed at him, "you guys scared him. He's all wide-eyed."

"Don't think that was us," Clara shook her head, "it was you, Cianna. Sykes," Clara reached her hand over the table and tapped his fingers, getting him to look away from Cianna's dragon tattoo. "Everyone's joking, alright? It's just how they are. There's no bad blood."

"Huh?"

What's going on?

He couldn't even hear them anymore. The static filtered into the rest of his body, making him itch. He tried to scratch himself, subtly at first, but the more he touched, the more he craved it.

"Maybe he's jealous?" Diego let the idea slide out of his mouth. "She's out of your league, man. Look at him," Diego pointed as Sykes blindly turned to Cianna, his eyes glued to her tattoo. "He's going in for second. By God, he's a hungry dog! Someone stop him!"

"Give the man a break," Gilbert groaned, taking another shot. "If he wants to look he can look. It's a free world."

"You moron," Clara hissed. "I've had enough of you."

"Let them be," Cianna said, amused by it all. She leaned her cheek into her palm as she propped herself against the table on her elbow. "I don't mind being admired," she twirled the straw around with her finger.

"You damn couga—aaaaw!" Diego scowled, Clara's fingers pinching his ear.

No-no-no-no... he scratched more and more, *it just can't be can it? I mean, people have golden tattoos and—*

A sudden tremor came from his right. He put it off as another symptom of whatever it was that he was going through, spilling outward from within. Yet as he turned his head, he saw Cole, his legs shaking. He was biting his teeth and scratching his palms beneath the table. His eyes darted from drink to drink. His legs shook, his eyes bulged out.

"You alright?" Sykes asked him—at least he thought. He could not hear his own words. "You want to go out for a smoke?"

"This is a smoking area," Sykes assumed Cole said as he read his lips.

"I know," he then responded, "but the air outside is nicer."

Cole looked up at him. His leg was jittery as well.

"I don't smo—"

"Me neither," Sykes got up either way, "but I could use one right now. Are you coming?"

Buzz after crackle after buzz. All inside of his body.

Cole looked around the table, confused. Diego was busy whispering something to Clara whilst she stared right at Sykes' back as he pulled away. She then looked at Cole as he got up, asked him *what's going on?* with a glance, but he turned and went after Sykes.

Sykes sat down on the curb. The noise wasn't any more subdued outside, but without the extra chatter and music, he could hear a little better.

"It's chilly out here," Cole came and sat down next to him.

"Yeah."

"You know I really don't like it when people pity me."

Sykes turned to him.

"That's why we're out here, right? You saw me struggling."

Sykes shrugged. "It's a little more selfish than that."

"How?"

"I wanted out, too. It was a little much."

"Ah," Cole sighed, "yes, they can be like that."

Sykes took out the packet of smokes and peeled the wrapper off. "You want one?"

"I thought you said you don't smoke."

Sykes shrugged. "Sometimes you need the numbness," he said, taking one out, placing the packet on the curb between them. "It's been 2 years for me."

"Never for me."

"Ah...shit."

"What?"

"I don't have a lighter," he groaned. "Whatever," he put the smoke between his lips and held it there, "this will do for now."

Silence sat down in between them, cozying up between their shoulders as they looked out at the city enveloped by night. Their eyes darted from window to window, some dark, some lit up as night owls got on with their duties.

"I quit drinking when Grigory died," Cole finally opened up.

"Did you?"

"We had a deal that we'll both try, you know. But it fell flat when he died. When he—" tears sprang up in his eyes.

"Here," Sykes handed him a smoke. "Just put it between your lips; it seems to help."

Cole stared at it for a moment before he complied.

"You can keep going if you want," Sykes told him.

"I don't know," Cole wiped his tears away, "there isn't much to say. It's just a pity. He shouldn't have died. It was no place for him to fight."

"Did he want to?"

"What?"

"Did he want to fight? That's my question. Was he forced to, or did he want to?"

"God, who knows?" Cole yowled, "The situation was dire and Icarus needed people. Sure, he offered up, but—" his lips squeezed at the smoke in his mouth, "who knows?"

"I'm sorry. You two sounded close."

"Yeah," he sighed, "we were."

"I'm sorry."

"Don't pity me," he gritted his teeth. "I hate that. Pity is for animals, not for people."

"Hey man," Sykes kept looking into the distance. His heartbeat was calm again, but his mind was running. "I'm not pitying you. I'm saying sorry for something else entirely. I'm saying sorry for being here."

"What?"

He shrugged. "I don't know. You must hate my guts, right? I just came in and filled that vacancy left behind by his passing, as if a human life is something of the sort that can be replaced. I'm sorry for that. It must be hard for you, seeing me there every day."

"It's not on you. It's on Icarus."

"Sure," Sykes nodded. "But that doesn't change much. I'm still there in his place. For you it's all and the same."

Cole didn't say much in response and Sykes took it as agreement.

"How could you forget a lighter?" he finally asked.

"What? I thought—" he stopped. "I'll go inside and borrow one."

"There's no need, really, it's just—"

"No, no," Sykes got to his feet. Just as he did, he spotted something strange in the corner of his eye.

It was brief, but he was certain it was there, in the alley. It was a stone mask.

Without thinking, he dashed towards it.

"Hey hey, Sykes...Sykes, where are you going?" Cole got to his feet. "What the hell?"

"Stop right there!" Sykes shouted, turning the corner and throwing himself into the dark alley.

"Sykes, what's going on?" Cole somehow caught up to him. Sykes was standing still, panting, staring into the alley, "what is it?" Cole tried to look on, but nothing was there. "What did you see? Sykes, come on," he grabbed at him, "talk to me. What the hell was that?"

"Where is he?" Sykes groaned, stepping further in, "let go, Cole. Someone was here—did you not see?" he looked exasperated, "someone...someone with a stone mask. They were here, watching us."

"I didn't see a thing. You're drunk, Sykes—I think."

"I'm not," he finally broke free and threw himself in the dark. "Do you have a light? He must be hiding here."

"Sykes, there's nobody…"

But Sykes ran deeper into the darkness. Cole looked back for a moment. "Oh God," and then he ran right after him.

Just then, the door of *The Underworld* burst open.

"What are you guys—"

Clara stepped out into the cold and was met with an empty street. There was no Sykes and no Cole.

She was alone and only brought her purse. She wobbled a bit on her heels as she paced back and forth, trying to see where they were.

To warm herself, she lit up a cigarette and waited.

"They shouldn't have gone far."

She considered sitting on the curb, but it looked too dirty for her nice clothes and she was in no mood to potentially throw them in the wash at home.

Clara was watching the smoke trail upwards and disappear into the night sky as shouting erupted out of an alley. She turned her head towards it. As the shouting continued, she got closer to the door, placing her hand on it and ready to go inside, but then, Cole burst out of the alley, dragging a frantic Sykes along with him.

"Christ almighty, would you calm down?!" Cole continued to shout, "there's nobody there! There's no dead body."

"But the blood…" Sykes gasped.

"There's no blood, Sykes! There's no blood, dammit! Look," Cole grabbed Sykes' hand, interlocking their fingers, "look at me!" he shouted, "there's no blood. Look at my hands, they are clean!"

Sykes' eyes were wide. His head shook, slowly at first.

"No-no-no," he said, "I swear...I..."

"Guys, what the hell?" Clara stepped away from the door. "What's going on?"

"Clara! Thank God, come help me out here, he's lost his mind!"

Clara took one last drag, flicked the smoke against the pavement and stomped on it with the tip of her pumps.

"Mr. St. Jane, hey, Mr. St. Jane, it's me!" she hurried forward, "what do I do, Cole? What's happening?"

"I don't know!" the poor man sounded distraught, "I don't fucking know!"

"Hey, hey," she added her hands over their own, clutching tightly. Theirs were warm with strain whilst hers were still cold, "talk to me."

"Mas—mas—"

"Mas *what?*"

"It's a masked man he keeps on talking about," Cole shook his head, "he keeps on repeating the same words. That and blood...and...ah...I don't know."

"Calm down, Cole. It's fine, I'm here. Here, take my purse and get us a cab."

"What?"

"Just get us a cab. I'll take him to my place."

"What about the others?"

She shook her head. "Just tell them the truth. He lost it a bit, maybe from the drink, and I took him to my place."

"Why not *his?*"

"He's in no shape to tell us his address."

"Well don't you know it from when you recruited him?"

"What do you think I am, a computer? Do you know how many addresses I go through daily?" she groaned, "come on. And besides, look at him, we can't leave him on his own."

"Authorities?"

"Be real, Cole!" she hissed, "just get the damn phone out!" Sykes jolted as she raised her voice. "Easy, easy, I'm sorry. We'll be fine, we're going home."

"Home?" he looked up at her, "no-no. The blood—the...Vulcan...my baby..."

"No no," she shushed him as Cole rummaged through her purse.

"Where the fuck is your phone you women and your pur—found it! Getting one now."

"Hey...hey, easy," she assured him, "We're just calling a cab, okay?"

"I need to go back," he gritted his teeth.

"Back where?" she asked, turning her head to Cole. "The cab?" she whispered.

"Two minutes."

"Back in there," Sykes pushed, "I'm not drunk, Clara. Just let me—"

"You *can't* go anywhere. We're going home."

"But...the mask..."

"We'll talk about the mask when you feel better," she sighed. "You're much too dru—angry, now."

The cab pulled up to the curb.

"Alright, that's us," she told him.

"Are you fine, Clara?"

"Yes, yes, I can handle him."

"Alright. By God call if anything happens, okay? I'll let the others know."

"Yeah...sure."

The booth was rowdier than before as Cole got back, sitting down silently and waiting for the right moment to speak up.

"What happened to you?" Gilbert nudged him. He reeked of alcohol. "Hey, guys," he raised his empty glass, drawing their attention, "something's wrong with Cole."

The table slowly quieted down as they turned to him.

Cole shook his head. "Nothing's wrong with me. Something happened with Sykes, though."

"Huh? What?" Diego was confused, "where's Clara?"

"She took him to her place."

Gilbert snickered, looking at Diego. A smirk started to appear on the man's face as well.

"It's not funny!" Cole harked, "alright? It's not. It was bad," he shook his head, "he went—he went—"

"Take your time," Kashmere assured him in a gentle tone.

"Poor Cole," Cianna whispered in her ear.

"Yeah," she nodded.

"Hey why do you have a cigarette in your hand?" Gilbert asked him.

"Oh..." Cole placed it on the table before him.

"Awh God it's all crumpled up. You people," Diego tutted. "Christ would you spit it out already?"

Cole lifted his brows and shoulders in a simultaneous confusion. "I just don't know. He was blabbering something about a masked figure in the alley," he said.

Gilbert sat up, wiping a drunken fog away from his eyes.

"What sort of masked figure?" Cianna asked. "Did he tell you?"

"Yeah, did he?" Diego leaned over, "God this is interesting."

"No. He just went crazy and chased after it but that *it* when I got there was nothing, it didn't exist. I don't know. He said something about *blood* too, *blood* on his hands."

"Did he now?" Diego narrowed his eyes, leaning right back. "How interesting."

"What else did he say about the mask?" Cianna pushed, "nothing?"

Gilbert threw a glance her way but said nothing.

Cole shook his head. "He looked so scared and lost...but...I don't know, there was...there was bloodlust there too, behind his eyes. That wasn't normal."

"Looks like we got ourselves a proper sicko on our hands, huh?" Gilbert cackled, "well," he groaned, "I guess there's nothing we can do about it now. He's in Clara's hands for tonight. We'll see what the matter is tomorrow—or Monday, at worst."

"Yeah," Cole nodded, sinking back into his own thoughts as the table returned to its chatter and joy as if his words had meant nothing at all.

Arthur jumped down from the wall.

"Come back here!" he heard from the other side.

"Sykes, calm down, what the hell?!"

"Fucking lunatics," Arhtur walked away, muttering to himself, "what the hell's wrong with these people?"

He slowly but carefully traced his way back, wasting some time to ensure that the two which spotted him were no longer outside the bar. He had to walk down one block before he turned and looped around, finding his car.

It was parked down another alley, empty, dark, deserted. Just like the one he had decided to waste some time in.

He looked inside the car, checking both the back and front and the trunk.

"No stragglers," he nodded. "Good."

He then peeled the skin of his left hand back and placed it against the door-frame, the gaping barrel pulsating with waves once more like before. The car started to bend like rubber before it sucked like spaghetti straight into his palm. He then folded the skin over the exo-skeleton underneath, arranged his suit, then went out of the alley, checking for prying eyes.

Once secure, he took a look at his watch, shaking his head.

"Shit," he hissed.

Without missing another beat, he stuck his hand in his suit coat pocket, removing a stone device from it. He clutched it in his palm, pulsating his waves over it. Instead of it bending and fraying out like loose fabric, the stone *beeped*, coming on, a blue light emanating from it, tinging the darkness.

Arthur turned the stone, pressing it against the alley wall. He twisted the device and with a *click* a perfectly circular hole opened up in the wall. Like a door, Arthur pulled it open and stepped through.

The hole closed behind him, leaving no trace.

The world at first is all but a blur. The limbs are heavy, confused, lost. He sits up and looks around. He is on the floor—no. There is no carpet, no floorboard. There is only cement under him.

There is blood everywhere. People are screaming his name.

'Mr. St. Jane! Mr. St. Jane! Mr. St. Jane! Mr. St. Jane! Mr. St. Jane!'

Over and over again.

Everyone seems distressed. He can feel that distress washing over him. He takes it as his own.

The world shakes. There are flashes of light and more blood. Shockwaves; more blood.

A butterfly flutters in his field of vision. It is blurred at first and then it comes and rests on his nose. A moment of serenity.

Blood trickles down the wings of the butterfly. Startled, the man tries to move. He cannot. The blood wraps around his head like a cocoon, trapping him, blinding him, taking him away.

The voices call again, but they are distant now. Sykes is going far away.

Three black BMWs pulled up to the curb, stopping their engines at once. One stone-masked figure stepped out of each.

All the doors shut at the exact same moment and they stepped on the pavement at the exact same time, converging into a circle with a set distance between shoulders.

Everything was in order; everything but *one* thing.

"Is it here, you're sure of it?" one of the figures asked. The stone mask consisted of a collage of butterflies, flying around.

Another, tallest of the lot, with such engravings on his mask that it resembled a fresh skull, checked his wristwatch.

"I'm getting pinged from here, yes."

"Why three of us?" another asked. Streaks of lightning covered his face. His eye slits were carved out in the same lightning-bolt design "We've got quite the firepower. Is it the real deal?"

"Arthur is busy," the tall one said. "He's getting an earful, so they sent us."

"The big shot?"

"The big shot."

"Tsk," Butterfly spat. As they talked, they didn't move any parts of their bodies. Only Skull checked his wrist every now and then. "Do we go up?"

"Yeah, do we go?" Lightning asked.

"And if we go, how do we do it? All calm and dandy? Do we kick down the door?"

Skull shook his head. "We knock."

"Knock? What are we knocking for? We know it's in there."

"There's nothing masking our presence. We *must* be calm," Skull sighed.

"And dandy," Butterfly added.

"And dandy, sure," Skull agreed.

"Then why three of us?"

"Yeah, why, boss?"

"I'm not your boss," he checked his watch again. It beeped more and more. "Come on."

He broke from the group and led the way to the entrance in the block. He made way for Lightning to reach his palm over the key-scanner. It beeped and the door opened.

Skull pulled the door open and led the way into the block.

"Can you tell us, then? Why we're 3?"

Skull tutted, then growled, then decided to actually tell them.

"We can never be sure that they will be as dandy and calm with us as we would like to be with them," he said, "Capeesh?"

The other two nodded and went up the steps towards the 7th floor; adverse to the elevators.

"Mr. St. Jane, wake up!"

His whole body shook awake. He found himself sitting down, still dressed.

"What?" he looked confused.

"God," she sighed, "you were howling."

"I...I was?"

Clara was hunched over him. She was wearing nothing but an oversized shirt.

Clara did not see where his eyes focused first.

She sighed and straightened herself. "I'm glad I got you awake."

"Y-yeah," he nodded. "Can you tell me—I mean, wh-what happened? Where am I?"

"Hmmm..."

"What time is it?"

"It's 2 in the morning," she yawned. "I took you to my place. You got drunk—or something—and started causing a ruckus."

"Oh...I'm sorry."

"No, it's fine."

"I should probably go," he grunted, trying to get up.

He didn't feel drunk at all.

His eyes still fixated on her. He couldn't take them away. He could barely see her outline as all the blinds were pulled. Only an odd, blue light illuminated her from somewhere down below—*from where?*

"Maybe," she agreed, "but you can also stay."

"I—I don't know."

"What's that in your hand, if you don't mind? It's been beeping for a while."

Sykes looked down. Clutched in his right hand was the stone device. The swirls were growing blue, brighter than ever before.

His eyes widened.

"Mr. St. Jane?" her tone was worried. "Did I ask something wrong?"

He put the stone aside. The light dimmed out.

"No, it's just—"

A knock came on the door. He looked up at her but Clara's head turned.

"Stay here," she hushed and stepped towards the door. She didn't bother to put anything else on. He followed her closely.

For some reason, his heart started to pound. He took a look at the device again as another knock came at the door.

Clara looked through the peep-hole. 3 stone-masked figures, dressed in white suits stood there waiting. One of them—the tallest—held his wrist up to his slits.

"The signal's disappeared," she heard him say.

"Do you think they caught onto us?" another voice asked from behind, coming from a Butterfly mask.

"No. They're in there."

The tall man knocked again.

"How do you know, boss?"

"I can hear a heart-beat on the other side of the door. Please," he cleared his throat, "come out, we just want to talk."

Clara stepped away, ran through the room and stood right before Sykes.

"You've got some explaining to do," she uttered through gritted teeth. Her breathing was heavy.

"What?"

"There are 3 people outside of my door, Mr. St. Jane."

"Okay, an—"

"They're wearing masks, *stone* masks," she spat. "Who..." she asked, stammered, then got the strength to try it again. "Who is outside my door?"

His eyes widened so much that she could see them in the dark.

"Look, I *know,* okay, that this might be a lot to you. I mean...that...fit back at *The Underground*, you mentioned them...you mentioned blood. You looked scared, Mr. St. Jane. I'm scared too, now. *Who* are they?"

Sykes shook his head.

"Are you sure they're here?" he asked.

"What, do you think I'm blind, or-or lying? *Who* are they?"

He shrugged. "I don't know, Clara, but you need to contact Gilbert right away."

He stood up and made his way towards the door, slowly.

"What? Gilbert?" she turned, hissing after him.

"If my hunch is correct, they're all extremely powerful Crafters," he said. "I...I barely handled one and that was a fluke."

"You *handled* one?" she sounded confused, "Syke—aaaah!"

She yelped as the light knocking on the door turned into bangs.

"Ms or Mrs. Occupant, we know you are in there. We've tried to be calm and dandy but you are giving us no choice. I will bang on this door three more times, if the door is not open by then, I will kick it down and this matter won't be calm nor dandy any more."

She looked towards Sykes.

The first bang came.

"Where are you going? Get away from there," she hissed, "get back here, are you out of your mind? I am calling Icarus right this moment! Get *back* here, Mr. St. Jane."

He lifted his finger. He was shaking all over—yet he knew what that meant for him; what he could do with that fear.

He paced closer to the door, standing tall before it as he looked through the peephole.

The second bang came as he peered through.

The three figures stood there, still, like statues. He recognized neither of them

Sykes looked carefully and placed his hand on the door, his fingers clawed. His heart was thumping fast enough for him to know that he was truthfully mortified.

He closed his eyes, focusing it all in his palm. He did it before, he could do it again.

"Mr. St. Jane, I'm calling—"

There wasn't a third bang.

Instead, the door blew off its hinges and propelled Sykes backwards, slamming him against the wall.

"Mr. St. Jane!"

"Coming through," the Skull said, "hey," as he turned towards Lightning, "you check the hall and make sure no one opens their doors."

Lightning nodded, retreating from the door.

"So, it was you that was trying to kill me?" he lifted the door off Sykes and crouched in front of him. "Is it you with the device as well? I can tell you're not gonna talk," he groaned and stood up, "leave him for now—all he's got is intent and fear. I can't sense anything else."

He kicked some of the splinters aside and stepped into the dark. He didn't seem to need the light to see as he manoeuvred with ease around the house.

"You," he pointed at Clara, "do you know anything about this device? It's a square, stone, lights up blue. Any clue?"

"Get out of my house!" she puffed.

"Easy now. There's no need to get violent."

"Boss," Butterfly chuckled at the door, about to step in, "picking on a woman is not calm or dandy at all."

"What else am I to do?"

"I don't know, just—huh?" Butterfly looked down. Sykes clutched his ankle with his right hand. "What are you, let go—"

Butterfly kicked away, but just as he did, his eyes witnessed the birth of a black ball in the palm of his captor. It formed and swallowed his whole foot and ankle as he kicked away.

"Fuck!" he roared. Blood splattered all over the walls. "Shit, Hect—fuck, boss, I need help. This is not dandy at all!"

"Just fix it yourself," Skull grimaced. "Now, *lady,*" he paced around the room some more, getting close to Clara. "You're the first heart-beat I felt. It's very distinct. You're very scared, I can tell. Don't be—that whole thing," he waved behind himself, "my friend is a little messy. We don't want to hurt you—this has *nothing* to do with you or your friend/relative/romantic partner. It's strictly business. One of our devices is missing, look," he pointed the watch to her face, "you probably can't see cause it's dark. We *need* this device. I am sure it's come into your hands by complete mistake. Someone as—" he stopped, looked at her a moment, "pardon me, *as wea—*"

She clutched her fist and swung.

"Swing and a miss," he said in a calm tone, holding onto her wrist, "or rather, a blo—"

Her eyes narrowed as sweat accumulated on her brow, her stare burrowing through his mask and right into his head.

How interesting; what is thi—*Stop talking. Be quiet, I'm looking for something.* **What is your Major? Psychology?** *Who do you work for?* **Does this usually work for you—this whole interrogation thing? It doesn't seem that fleshed out, lady. It's not very nice. I tried to be dandy earlier and not insult you, but now, you're**—*shut up and answer me who are you what do you want and who do you work for? Who sent you*—**in my head and I don't appreciate that one bit. You tricked me, you see, and that is not dandy—we don't consider it that way. You are so weak that I couldn't even sense your Craft.** *I'll stay in here until you answer me.* **You think you're in here out of your own strength? Ha! Sure, you entered my mind, but don't be fooled. I can kick you out at any moment. I won't. I won't, because the thing with weak Psychology Crafters is that they don't know how to close the channel of communication, let's see, shall I take a visit to you—**

Clara yanked her arm away, severing the connection.

"C-Crafter, I assume?" he spat at her with disgust. "Your friend over by the door seems a little stronger, he's got my friend in a pinch. I would've expected him to be by my side by now.

Nuh-uh," he moved over as Clara tried to look over his shoulder, "that's their business. We have our own. The device, please."

"I don't know of any device."

"You're lying. I can tell you're lying because of your heartbeat. Don't lie to me. Tell me," he nodded his skull-mask at her, "is it in this room? Good, thank you for that," he nodded, "your heart beat is all I need."

She tried to hit him again, but this time he simply caught her hand by pinching her wrist, digging his finger into her muscles.

Clara didn't understand at first. Then, her muscles contracted all at once—her heart felt as if it was going to burst and she flew backwards, banging into the wall, cracking it.

She thudded onto the floor.

"Hurting women is not dandy at all. Excuse me," he stepped over her.

She tried to reach for him but couldn't move. Skull calmly searched around for the device, not caring for anything happening in his surroundings.

Sykes pushed the door off himself and stood up. Butterfly was dragging himself away, blood trailing behind his maimed ankle. There seemed to be no real distress in his movements as he reached his hand for his foot. The butterfly etchings on his mask turned pink.

A light of similar colour then coursed down his arm, towards his ankle, where two pink butterflies materialised out of thin air.

Sykes stopped for a moment, startled by the sudden burst of pink light, but also by what was happening with the butterflies themselves.

They attached to the man's ankle and began to suck up the blood leaking out of it until their bodies grew fat and round.

They grew a little more and—*POP*—they burst.

The blood did not splatter in all directions like before. Instead, it was concentrated around the ankle and turned into silk-like threads. A mummified red cocoon stood like a peg instead of the man's foot.

He pushed himself further away from Sykes and stood up, limping a bit.

"Now," he loosened his tie. "There was no need for that, was there? Before we continue, let me ask. How quickly do you want to die?"

"Wh-what?" Sykes stammered.

"Heh," Butterfly suddenly stepped forward. In the same motion, he removed the tie from around his neck completely and, holding onto it, he hurled one end forward.

The mask etchings turned orange. The light surged down his arm and tie, reaching the tip just as it hit against Sykes.

Two already fattened, orange butterflies, pushed out of the tie, right next to Sykes. They fizzed for a moment, and, as Sykes reached his hand up to protect himself, they exploded.

The boom rattled the entire apartment, lighting it up as the explosion propelled Sykes backwards. He slammed into the wall, putting a hole in it as all the glass panes shattered, shards flying in all directions.

"Already?" Skull called, "what's gotten into you?"

"This one's a tough cookie, boss," Butterfly wrapped the tie around his fist. "Look at him. He's still standing after that. What's with him? You said nothing about a guy like him."

Skull stood still for a moment, looking at Sykes shaking off the attack. His pants were burnt through and his exposed shins scorched, but the rest of him seemed pretty intact.

"Because there was nothing to say before," Skull shrugged, "now, he's seemed to awaken some power. What are the odds-eh? To get an epiphany when we barge in. Suppose the world works in mysterious ways. Say, you got him, yes?"

"Of course, who do you think—"

As soon as Sykes got to his feet, he dashed out of the apartment.

"Hey, where are you—" Butterfly stepped forward. The cocoon on his foot slowly started to take the shape of a proper ankle and foot. It wasn't quite there yet, so his movement was staggered as he ran after Sykes, "you know, man, leaving a woman behind with two guys is not dandy at—uuggh—"

As he stepped into the hall, Sykes tackled him from around the bend. He had been waiting, pressed to the wall. As he floored him, he pressed his clawed hand against his ribs and right away the black ball started to swirl out, swallowing his body.

"Fuuuuuck!" blood splattered from beneath his mask. The man had managed to punch out with his tie. His punch was weakened, his vitals much more so. Only one orange butterfly materialised, landing on Sykes' shoulder. "Boom!" the man said, and the butterfly exploded.

It sent Sykes flying backwards. His ears rang incessantly.

He could smell the burn on his own skin and hair. He was dazed, barely able to move.

He was laid flat on his back, his head against the wall. Dust trickled down over his body from the cracks in the wall. He tried to get up, but his body hurt too much.

Butterfly laid there, too, his guts spilling out. His hand moved towards his torn body. His whole left side was gone. His movements were growing weaker and weaker.

Yes, Sykes thought to himself, *fuck you!*

That is when Skull stepped out of the apartment.

"Sheesh," he groaned, looking towards Sykes at first. "I found it," he lifted the device. "And from it, I can sense the same power that you emanate. Tell me, do you have anything to do with the disappearance of one of our people?"

As he spoke, he stepped towards Butterfly. He crouched down and pressed his hand against his head.

"You're a total mess," Skull croaked. "How's that dandy at all? How can you get bested by someone so weak?"

Butterfly said nothing at first. His hand then began to move.

"Are you up and running?" Skull asked. "Come on, can you Craft?"

"Y-yeah."

"Do it, then. We have to go. Where's Lightning?" Skull looked up. The third man was nowhere to be seen.

Pink butterflies materialized and coated all of the man's body.

Skull made his way to Sykes.

"Now what do we do with you, huh, I wonder?"

Sykes tried to pull away. His jaw hurt, but the words he wanted to say were there, on his tongue and lips, and he pushed through the pain.

"Wh-what," he coughed, "what did you do to Cl-Clara?"

"Is that her name?" he asked. "I stopped her heart," he said, matter-of-factly.

"You *what?!*" Sykes howled.

"Easy now," the man chuckled, "I'm just kidding. Gosh, your heart is pounding fast."

"You—you killed...you killed her," Sykes spat.

"Can't you hear that I didn't? Killing women is not in my style, especially innocent, weak ones. She had nothing to do with this. You dragged her into it, didn't you?"

"I—"

"You could've held onto the device yourself and—nope," Skull suddenly stepped on his wrist, "that's a dangerous hand. I ain't lettin' you use it. Now listen to me," he crouched, "I have reason to believe you are involved in this little incident the organization I work for is currently occupying itself with. What do you have to say about that?"

"I...I don't have—"

"Yeah, well." Skull shrugged, "if you really are innocent, that is for us to decide later. For now," Skull stood, looking back. "You up?"

"Yeah."

"Cocoon this guy."

Butterfly dragged himself to his feet. The whole left side of his body was a misshapen bloody cocoon, slowly building itself back. He was moving slowly, not wanting to disrupt the recovery of his insides, either way, he lifted an arm and pointed his finger at Sykes.

"His hand," Butterfly groaned, "it's gonna be trouble, boss. I won't be able to hold him in here if he can make use of it."

"Smart," Skull tapped the side of his mask.

He pushed down on his wrist even harder with one foot as he swung the other through the air, kicking at his hand—hard and fast—snapping his wrist.

"AAAAAAAAAAAAAAAAAAAAAAAAAARGH!"

"It had to be done," he excused himself, "now, the cocoon."

Sykes writhed around on the floor, screaming at the top of his lungs as spittle frothed up around his mouth. He saw in his frantic panic multiple pink butterflies coming for him.

They rested on his body and expanded, exploding once they reached their limits and starting to spread their blood silken threads all over his body, wrapping him up in a giant cocoon until he was completely engulfed.

"That's good enough," Skull groaned. "Pick him up, we're getting back to our cars as soon as we find Lightning."

Skull moved first, Butterfly following him, dragging the cocoon after him. There was no sign of struggle from within—the whole body was encased, leaving it no space.

As they passed by a door, it suddenly opened. Skull and Butterfly stopped, ready to explain themselves.

Yet it was only Lightning stepping out of someone else's apartment.

"Oh," Lighting gasped, "my bad, guys. I was just checking the place. Holy crap," he whistled, looking at the blood on the walls;

the cracks in the ceiling and the cocoon behind Butterfly. "What the hell happened?"

"Pushback," Skull shrugged. "Let's go, we've overstayed our welcome."

"Gonna be a lot of clean-up to do, huh, boss?"

"A lot of chewing out by the higher-ups as well," Butterfly added, dragging the cocoon past Lightning.

Lightning picked up the other end of it, helping him carry it down the steps.

"Do you think it's going to get reported to *them*?" Butterfly asked, a shudder in his voice.

Skull stopped, turned, looked up at them from below.

"Don't say stupid things," he growled, "if it gets to *them*, we're all fucked."

They all nodded, descending the steps. Some doors were open, people's heads poking out, confused. As they saw the blood on their suits and the cocoon getting carried by the men, some whimpered and shouted, some asked questions.

Of course, they were left unanswered.

Most doors banged shut as people retreated inside, getting as far away as possible. Some called the police.

The three men did not hurry.

The entrance into *The Underground* was crowded as people waited for their cabs to come pick them up.

"Man," Diego yawned, "alcohol really doesn't do it for me anymore."

"It's cause you're too damn big. Look at you."

Diego cackled and hit Gilbert over the shoulder. "What about you, then, huh?"

"Good liver," he tapped it with his hand.

"Any news on Clara and Sykes?" Kashmere asked.

Diego shrugged.

"Probably going at it," Gilbert said.

Cole and Kashmere glared at him.

"I don't know, it seemed—"

Their phones started to buzz all at once. They looked at one another, already on alert. They took them out of their pockets and purses and placed them to their ears.

The same voice spoke out in all of them.

"Clara's residence, *now*. She's been hit, *hard*. They took our Muffin Man."

"Shit!" Diego growled. "Do we have permi—"

"I have requested it from the government. It takes a while for permission to come in, as you know. Still," the man's voice was deep and gloomy, "you are free to use your powers to get there as fast as possible."

"Director, that—"

"I said you are *free* to use your powers. I will take care of any backlash. You go and save our agents. I won't lose any more of them. Also," he added, right before he cut the call, "I'm alerting the Upper Six."

"It's that bad?" Diego asked.

The line cut. The agents looked at one another, placing their phones back in their pockets. They looked at one another and understood.

CHAPTER EIGHT

The three masked men were taking the last steps down into the lobby.

"I didn't even ask you, boss, did you find the device?"

"Why do you think we left already?" Skull asked. "Enough stupid questions, though. Let's just get out of here."

As they stepped into the lobby, the elevator *dinged*.

"Ah," Skull smiled. "We have a visitor."

The elevator doors parted.

"Clara, was it?" Skull asked, "I learned your na—"

Clara had an SMG in her hand and bands of ammunition strapped around her. Her eyes scanned the lobby.

Once done, she pulled the trigger.

The bullets soared right towards the three targets. She aimed for their heads at first, yet as soon as the first bullet clinked against Skull's mask, not even making a dent, she lowered her weapon and aimed for their bodies. Two bullets hit the Skull in the shoulder. The Butterfly's left side had nearly recovered, yet as he started to run out of the apartment block, he was caught in the ribs, spluttering blood everywhere.

Lightning had not been hit at all.

Come on, you assholes, she thought, her body rattling as she held the trigger down. *Give him back!*

Bullets tore through the air, hitting against windows. Millions of shards flew in all directions. Skull suddenly stepped aside, making way for the other two.

"You two go," Skull shouted over the gun-fire. Yet before his next words came, it stopped. "I will take care of her."

Shit.

Clara stepped back into the lift, reloading her SMG and continuing to fire. At first, Skull didn't trouble himself too much. He held his hand lifted before him, powerful shock waves emanating from it, blocking the bullets, crushing them before they reached him.

"You going to do this all night, Clara?" he asked.

He stood his ground, waiting for her to reload once more. As soon as the gun *clicked* with an empty clip, he lowered his arm.

Skull darted forward.

*Here I go...*she thought

He had managed three steps by the time she began firing again. She held the SMG with one hand whilst she pressed the button to a random higher floor with the other hand.

Skull raised his palm once more. Once more he remained still.

"Can't move whilst doing that or what?" she shouted, reaching her hand behind her back. Strapped to the hem of her underwear (she hadn't had the time to change from her sleeping attire) there was a metal ball. The word *ICARUS* wrapped around it. She unstrapped it, pressed the button on top and threw it at his feet.

In the clamour of bullets and with his attention concentrated on his palm, he had not noticed it. Her bullets stopped right as the door was about to close.

"Asshole," she spat as the elevator door closed, taking her away.

It was then, in the silence, that he heard the beeping. He looked down at the ball, growing red, blinking and then—

BOOM!

In the meantime, on the other side of Chives Dale, Diego's large body leaned out the back-window of a cab, his clothes fluttering in the wind.

"Shit, hold me properly, dammit!" Diego roared.

His Crafter Log floated right next to him, following the speed of the car as the chains crinkled in the air.

"Sir..." the driver looked cautiously back at Diego.

Kashmere was in the front seat, her hand on the driver's shoulder.

"It's all okay," she tried to soothe him, "we're Crafters, like I said. We work for Icarus. There's nothing to worry about."

"Me no care! I have childs!"

"We won't harm your children," she sighed. "No one will! Guys," she turned in her seat, "it's not working. He won't listen."

"Just keep talking to him!" Gilbert shouted from the back seat. The wind was much too loud as he held onto one of Diego's thick legs.

Cole held onto the other.

"Please, sir," the driver kept turning his head, "ple—"

"Just drive straight, man, straight," Gilbert groaned, "is it that hard?!"

"Shut up, Gilbert! Stop scaring him!"

"He's going to make us late! Come on!"

In a desperate attempt, Kashmere took out her ID.

"Look," she pointed, "hey," and then clicked her fingers to get his attention. "Official Crafter!"

"No care!" he shook. "This too much! I get in trouble"

"WE ARE **THE** TROUBLE, ASSHOLE!" Gilbert roared from the backseat, "no cop will stop you! DRIVE!"

The driver peered through the rear-view mirror.

"**VROOOM!**" Gilbert roared, "**VROOM or kaput!**"

At the sound of the word *kaput*, the driver's eyes widened.

"Don't threaten him!" Kashmere slapped his shoulder.

Yet the car sped up, the man's eyes back on the road. Not for long, though, as a building fast approached.

"LEFT, RIGHT?!"

"Straight!" Gilbert shouted.

"WHAT?!"

"STRAIGHT OR KAPUT!"

"BUT BUILDING, SIR!"

"*KAPUT, YOU HEAR? KAPUT!*" howled Gilbert.

The driver whimpered and closed his eyes. His hands clutched at the wheel and his foot, against all common-sense, pressed onto the gas pedal.

Outside, as the car sped up more and more, the wind picked up speed, hitting against Diego's face. His hair got ruffled by the wind as he seemed to draw something out of the Log.

He rolled it around his fingers, then hurled the invisible material at the ground in front of him. Then, in his own time, he twisted his hand and made a motion as if to order something to rise up from the dead.

The smell of freshly-rained-on-cement filled the car as hardened cement started to materialise beneath the car's wheels, lifting it up as it formed a ramp.

"Aaaah!" the driver shouted, sensing his car starting to lean.

"Calm down!" Gilbert shouted, "and more on the gas, man, we ain't going to make it if you pussy out on it!"

"Yes, sir, yes,!"

Gilbert held onto Diego's leg and turned his head back, looking through the rear-window. Cianna had insisted on getting her own cab. For a moment, he was concerned, yet as he looked on, he saw the headlights of her cab coming right after them, ascending the slope which led far up past the tall buildings of Chives Dale.

The driver's eyes were wide open now. He found himself on top of the world, Humphrey's Peak and the whole mountain range right before him.

"VROOM VROOM!" Gilbert repeated, rattling him.

The driver nodded, his foot heavy against the gas pedal.

"Still no response from Clara?" Cole asked.

"No," Kashmere muttered, checking her phone.

"Can we go faster?!" Gilbert roared.

The driver said nothing.

Clara felt the explosion from two floors up.

God I hope that got him, she thought, reloading the SMG.

Doors opened. People poked their heads out and stared at her.

SMG in hand, only a loose shirt on and nothing else.

"Who the hell are you?" a man asked.

"Just get inside," she shouted, "I'm with ICARUS!"

Whispers passed from one door to the other.

I don't have time for this, she thought, breaking into a run as her bare feet clapped against the floor.

She took the stairs down towards the lobby, keeping the SMG close to her body. Approaching the lobby, she slowed her pace and clutched the SMG tighter.

A cloud of dust floated lazily over the entire room, masking everything.

Careful now. He catches you unaware, you're dead. God—where is everyone? What's taking so long?

Her bare feet brushed against debris.

*I just have to find Sykes. That's all. This time—I can do it. I don't have to be a fighting type, but I can still protect. I **have** to.*

Shards of glass pierced her soles, yet she did not wince. She stepped carefully, in need of total silence. The air was thick with a choking scent. She tried to breathe as little as possible as she scanned the room through the misty cloud.

Just be quick, she talked to herself, *you see him, you shoot. No questions, only action. Remember...remember...God just remember.*

Her throat dried up. The drumming of her pulse seemed to scratch against it.

Her hands slipped with sweat, making her readjust her grip, over and over.

One foot in front of the other.

One step, then another—then *flesh*. It brushed against her ankle. She spun quickly, pointing the gun at the ground, her finger shaking over the trigger.

She did not shoot. It was only a foot. Somehow, the metallic scent of blood managed to sneak its way into her nose.

Some damage, good.

Instinctually, she looked upwards. If the foot was there, *some* part of the body needed to be somewhere on the ceiling as well.

Yet there wasn't. She paced around some more, only getting two more steps in before she heard a groan.

It came from her left.

She turned and paced carefully. She saw the rest of the body plastered against the wall. The suit was torn off and dirtied; the mask was perfectly intact.

Skull didn't seem to hear her approach. She got close to him, close enough to press the muzzle of the SMG against his chest, right over his heart, without him even spotting here.

"You're in bad shape," she muttered. "Couldn't spot my pulse?"

"That you, Clara?"

"*Don't* say my name," she pushed the muzzle against his chest a little harder.

Skull winced.

Clara moved her free hand towards his mask. As her fingers grazed it, his own twitched. She caught onto the movement, and, in an instant, she pulled the muzzle from his chest, firing two bullets down into his wrist.

"Aaah..." he groaned, his hand falling limp. "Was that—necessary?"

"I'd say so," she nodded. "And just because you gave me cheek," she turned and shot his other wrist as well.

Another groan.

"You gonna try read my mind, Clara?"

She pressed the muzzle back against his chest, saying nothing.

"Oooh, you're smarter than that, are you?"

She ignored him, reaching her hand for his mask once more.

"There's no point taking that off," he said as soon as her fingers grazed it again. "I mean it."

"Shut up," she muttered, looking for a way to peel it off.

"It's just *style*, I promise you," he gave a wet cough.

She searched some more until she found a strap at the back of his head.

"Come on," a deep breath filled his lungs with a crackle and pop. "Do you really need to? It's not dandy at all, I promise you. Your friend," he sounded alert as soon as her fingers tightened on the clasp, "what if he's gone already? Eh? You're wasting your time with me here."

"You're not doing yourself any favours," she finally said, "talking all the time. Just be quiet."

"Heh-eh—" he tried to laugh, but it quickly turned into a laboured cough.

The mask *unclipped* yet still remained attached to his face. Slowly, she pulled it off with her fingers. As the dust cleared, the scent of blood grew even thicker.

"Jesus Christ," Clara groaned. Her throat tightened, her hands growing sweatier. "Who the hell did this to you?"

Skull's face was completely peeled.. All that remained of it was dry muscle and some of the skeleton, plus the eyes, large and round and bloodshot, staring right at her.

"It's part of the look," he cackled with his teeth completely exposed. Something turned in her stomach, making her look away. "And there's also a purpose."

"Purpose? What—what purpose?"

"In case *this* happens," he said. "In case our masks get pulled off. Nothing can identify us this way."

"You have teeth," she corrected, "and you have fingerprints."

Skull found the strength to laugh.

"What's so funny?" she asked, pushing the muzzle into his chest.

"You're a smart girl, right?" he asked. "You'll figure it out soon enough, I'm sure, so I'll just tell you. I want..." he hesitated, his round eyes analysing her face. "I want to see your face when I tell you."

"Tell me *what*?"

"Just look at my teeth, darling," Skull whispered. She wasn't sure whether he smiled or not, with the lips ripped off, it wasn't certain. "And look *closely*. You'll see this matter ain't dandy at all."

And so she looked. It took her a moment to realise, to put it together. His teeth were all of different shades and sizes, arranged haph-hazardly in his mouth.

"Thats..."

"I don't need to tell you not to bother with the prints, do I?"

"Who—"

"You know I won't answer that," he sighed. His eyes tried to roll into the back of his head, needing rest, but there were no lids to cover them. "Or anything else, for that matter. I'm done."

"You won't speak?" she asked. "Are you certain?"

"Certain."

Clara pressed the trigger. His body limped as the bullet pierced his heart. His skinned head fell forward, right on her shoulder. With a shudder, she nudged it back.

Now where's that thing? she searched his pockets. Her fingers touched the stone. *There we go,* she picked it out and stood up, stepping away.

She stood there a few moments, just to be sure that he didn't spring to life. Once certain, she lifted her hand to her face. It shook like crazy.

Calm down. You still have to get Sykes somehow.

In a dark room, only a set of blue lights could be seen, burning low.

"Kneel, Arthur," a mysterious voice demanded.

In the dark, the blue lights lowered.

"Where are you looking at?" the same voice boomed and the eyes turned towards the dark ground. "Good. Where is the device?"

"It seems it was not at the house we were told to retrieve.

"*What*? So you failed?"

"Perhaps," Arthur said, "but *perhaps* not."

The voice cackled in the dark until a hard, wet, cough took its place. Arthur listened to it all, unmoved.

"You are brave, Arthur."

"I know not of brevity."

"And a fool at the same time," the voice continued. "Don't pretend you possess no emotions. Your mind is quite developed; you have obtained an epiphany after all."

"But not emotion."

"Be it as you may," the mysterious voice groaned. "*What* is it you know?"

"Skull, Butterfly, and Lightning have been deployed."

"Correct," the voice confirmed.

"Have they succeeded?" Arthur asked.

"Skull is dead," the voice responded. "His signal is lost."

"Is he perhaps playing dead?"

"No. The signal has been gone too long; much longer than ever before. He is dead for sure. Killed by a lowly woman with a gun."

"A gun?" Arthur asked, surprised.

The voice broke out into laughter yet again. The sound surrounded Arthur, squeezing him in. "Look at you. One moment, you claim that you possess no emotion, yet now you sound as if your innards have been pulled out of you" the voice sounded pleased, "Cybress is one heck of a woman for creating you. Yes, indeed. *Listen,* Arthur. You are needed out there. Go before we are made fools of."

The blue specks of light looked forward.

"What about Cybress?"

"She is making her move," the voice assured him, "yet she has to be careful. She cannot be revealed."

"Then if she—"

"You *are* needed. I hear that those on Earth are sending some big players."

"This was meant to be a silent operation," Arthur said.

"You don't have to tell *me*," the voice growled, "leave it to humans to mess things up. Now," a blue circle swirled beneath Arthur's kneeled body, illuminating it, "be gone."

The swirls opened up, swallowing him up and taking him away.

"Boss sure is taking his time," Butterfly groaned. "I'm starting to think he's got done in."

"There were some strange noises coming outta there, huh?" Lightning wondered. "A few too many bullets for my liking."

"Is he dead you think?"

"Beats me," Lightning tapped his fingers on the hood of his car. "You got the cocoon in there?"

"Yup," Butterfly slapped the rear-door of his car. "All armed up, too."

"Great."

"What, you're thinking of going?" surprise crackled in Butterfly's voice.

"I mean..."

"Boss will be in a bad bad mood. He won't give us no noodles, you know?"

Lightning scratched the back of his head. "I hear you, man," he groaned, "I do. But...I don't know. I've got a bad feeling about this."

"I *hate* bad feelings."

"Tell me about it."

"Hey.."

"Yeah?" Lightning turned.

"Monica's gonna cook something for us."

"You think?" Lightning's voice showed hints of hope.

"I sure hope so. Come on, we can go and check. I am sure she can help us explain the situation to boss."

"If he's still alive."

"Yup yup, if that," Butterfly clicked his fingers, stepping into his car.

He placed the key in the ignition, yet stopped as soon as he heard an engine revving somewhere nearby.

He looked in his rearview mirror and saw that Lightning had still not started his.

"What in the—" Butterfly stepped back out, an incessant honking pulling at him.

"Butterfly..." Lighting called, he, too, out of his car, looking up. "We've got company, I say."

Butterfly laced his fingers and then cracked them. "Looks like it."

Diego jumped right out of the window as the cab began to skid on the normal road. His Log was no longer floating by him.

As the car came to a stop a little further off, the others came out too. As soon as the doors banged shut, the driver floored it.

"Where the hell is Cianna?" Gilbert asked. "Wasn't she right behind us?"

"Heeellllooooooooo," Butterfly shouted, "are you guys *that* preoccupied that you won't even bother with us?"

Gilbert had his hands in his pockets. He turned his head and scanned the two masked figures.

"Halloween's some ways off, pal," he hissed.

"Baha!" Butterfly rolled his head back, "a knee-slapper, that one! Surely! How great, Lightning. This one's a comedian!"

"I hate comedians," Lightning spat.

"Shit, for real? Why did you never tell me?"

Gilbert took one hand out of his pocket. He curled his index finger into his thumb, ready to shoot.

"Where are the two you attacked?"

"What's this guy talking about?" Lightning asked.

"Man," Butterfly turned, "you missed it all. There was this woman and—"

Gilbert shot his ray of light at Butterfly's forehead.

"Huh," Gilbert hummed as the shot reflected right off. "Sturdy mask."

"That wasn't dandy, man. You always give a warning before you attack!" Butterfly unrolled his tie, wrapping it around his fist.

"Says who?"

"Says *me*, asshole!" he roared, "now come here and fight like a man."

Gilbert placed his forefinger against his thumb once more. Butterfly dashed from the spot he was at, running in zig zags towards Gilbert.

The second flick shot the beam right through Butterfly's chest, making him stop his pursuit.

"You can't outrun my lasers, pal."

"Crap," Butterfly grimaced, "now I smell like a burnt pig!"

Gilbert flicked twice more. A beam caught Butterfly in his shoulder, the other in his abdomen.

"That's all?" Butterfly asked, his mask turning pink. Butter-flies started to flutter their wings over the holes in his body, stitching their wings together in order to heal his wounds. "You'll have to step it up, friend."

"We're not friends."

"Not yet, that's for sure," Butterfly cackled.

He picked up the pace, drawing closer as he unfurled the tie from around his fist. His mask glowed orange, the light spreading to the tie as it extended towards Gilbert.

"Gilbert! Diego shouted, clapping his hands together.

The road erupted out of the ground right in front of Gilbert, yet before it could harden, the night sky flashed a blinding white.

"Hi," Lightning said, suddenly appearing next to Diego.

"Shi—"

A strong, quick fist slammed into Diegos' ribs, propelling him through the air. He flew until he hit a distant building.

Kashmere grabbed onto Cole.

"Quick yellow, strong green," she whispered.

"What was that?" Lightning placed a hand to his ear, turning to them, "you want to be next? Fine."

The whole world lit up again and Lightning, under a second, crossed the distance and found himself with his fist pulled backwards. With the same speed, he rushed it forward, aiming for Kashmere's face.

Lightning's fist caved her face in. Soon, though, he found his whole arm had pushed through her head.

"Yeesh," he muttered, but then the whole of Kashmere's body melted into green and yellow paint. "What?" he turned on his feet. "What the hell? Where did they go?"

Kashemre came to a stop a little way off, right around a bend. Cole shuddered to his core.

"What's the matter with you?" she asked. "Can you not fight?"

"When could I ever?" he looked up. His eye were round and rheumy. "I...I let Grigory die."

"Oh...no...Cole..." she tried to find the words. "Now...now is not the time..."

Cole shook his head. "Kash," he looked at her. "Diego got *blasted*. What chance do we stand?"

"I don't know, Cole. I don't know and I don't care, alright? But whatever we can do, we *must* do. We can't make the same mistakes as before," she gripped his shoulder, "even if we fear repeating them. We—"

The sky lit up.

"There you are!" he zoomed right next to them, "nice trick. But how many—"

Once more his fist went right through her. The colours appeared and she was gone, together with Cole.

As she came to a stop, Cole looked around.

"You brought us back?!"

Kashmere pointed at the hole in the wall. "We need to help Diego," she said. "He is half of our fighting power right now."

"What about Gilbert?" Cole asked, "he—"

"He hasn't been punched through a building *yet*," Kashmere groaned, "Cole, come on, get it together!"

"What...what are you two bickering about?" Diego called from the other side of the wall. "It's not doing my ribs any good.

"Are they broken?" Kashmere rushed towards his side, "Cole," she looked up, *do something,* **please!***"*

Her eyes searched Cole thoroughly. He was much too distant, locked in a whole different world. No matter how much she tried, she found nothing.

"Cole," she placed her hand on his shoulder, "Cole…"

—

"…Cole, wake up, buddy, hey."

Cole's eyes are glued with sleep as he forces them open. He lifts his head from the table, dozens of papers sliding off him.

"Grigory?" he calls, as if uncertain.

"Who else, you doofus?" he leans in to kiss the side of his head. "I've brought you coffee."

"Oh…thanks."

"How much longer will you be?"

"I mean," Cole looks around at all the papers, "I'm…just scratching the surface."

Grigory's hands clutch his shoulders, giving them a good, comforting squeeze.

"They better promote you after this."

"It's *not* about that."

"You say that, but…"

"I mean it, Grigory," Cole turns. "I don't *want* Icarus to promote me. I want to find a *cure.*"

Like a ghost, Grigory slides down onto a chair next to him. He brings his legs together and places his feet on Cole's footrest.

"Is alcoholism really something you're willing to devote yourself to?"

"I've lost too many people to it," he mutters, shifting through some papers, his coffee untouched. "And the world *keeps* losing people to it. *Too* many."

"It loses people to other things, too."

"Sure," Cole nods, "but you don't see advertisements promoting shark attacks, or mass murders shelved in every damn store in the country."

"You're exaggerating, I mean—"

"I am *not!*" Cole slams his hand on the table. "And *even if* I am, it's my issue, I am allowed to blow it as far out of proportion as I want! No one, Grigory, no one in this damn world seeks to solve this problem, but everyone is aware of it! I hate that! I hate people that are aware of something that needs fixing, *right now,* and decide to let it slip."

"So you hate me?" Grigory pushes a strand of hair away from his eye so he can see better. "Is that it?"

"Don't be stupid," Cole shakes his head. "You know that's far from the truth."

"The whole world is like that, Cole," Grigory sighs. "You're alone in this."

"No, I'm not. Icarus..." he smiles, "Icarus stretches its wings wide, Grigory. Whatever they cast a shade over, they take care of—or at least *try* to. I've come to them with this issue and they are doing *everything*, and I mean, *everything* in their power to support me. It's a great place," he turns to him. "You should apply. I'm sure you'll get in."

"What would I even bring to a place like that? Are you serious?" Grigory laughs dismissively.

"You'd bring something of great importance."

"Oh yeah? What's that?"

"Yourself."

"Cole..."

—

"...Cole, Cole!" Kashmere shook him awake. His eyes suddenly grew into focus. "He *needs* your help."

"I'm sorry," Cole kneeled beside Diego. "I'm still finding it hard to think after ...you know."

"Don't worry, *amigo*," Diego smiled. "My brain's all mush, too."

Only now did Cole see just how bad the hit had been. Diego was amidst rubble, his large chest plagued by laboured breathing as blood trickled down his chin. An unknown white light flickered inside the building, another shot sparks.

"I assume broken ribs," Cole said, "and—"

"Just ribs," Diego smiled.

"You sure?"

"Yup."

"Just a second, then," Cole closed his fist, shaking it as if he was rolling dice, before he opened his palm. "Take this," he handed him a capsule. "It should help for a little while."

"How *little*? I'm a man all about large proportions."

"*Enough* for this battle."

"Now we're talking," Diego picked up the pill, popping it in his mouth. He crunched it with his teeth and gulped it down raw.

"Move your arm up and down. Once it stops hurting, it's safe to get up."

With a great deal of strain, Diego started moving his arm. Each span of it felt as if his ribs were getting ripped right out of him. Slowly, though, the pain faded, until nothing of it remained but a memory.

"All-fucking-right," he shot to his feet, rubble falling off him.

He stood there a moment, narrowing his eyes as he looked straight ahead. Reflecting in the darkened windows of buildings, were large explosions and brief flares of red light.

"That sleezy fucker's still kicking," he smiled, "good. Listen, you two," he looked down at them, standing a couple heads taller than them. "Those two masked shit-heads were *just* about to leave Clara's apartment, meaning they didn't get away with our Muffin Man, *or* with her. Alive, dead, they're still there, in that building, or in one of those damn *beamers*. I'm fresh now," he clenched his fist, no pain in his whole body, "and these two fucks are strong. It's not worth it you two getting into this. Leave it to me and Gilbert."

"Diego," Cole stepped forward, "we *must* do something."

"We *will*," Kashmere assured him. "We can look for Sykes and Clara as they fight."

"But—"

"Don't you *but* and *what if* me," Diego snapped. "Gilbert and I will handle our side, you handle yours. Deal?"

Cole hesitated.

"*Amigo,*" Diego clasped the top of Cole's head in his palm, ruffling his hair endearingly, "faith in your best buds should never waver. If I tell you all's well, all's well, even if it isn't, you understand? If you run around shitting your pants, you'll be a lot heavier, so do yourself a favour and keep those *pantalones* clean, yeah?"

"Fine," Cole nodded, "yeah, you're right. I'm sorry."

"Ah, it's nothing," Diego waved it off.

"Diego," Kashmere called.

"Hmmm?"

"Here," she placed her hands on his thick forearm. "*Strong Green, Quick Yellow — 100%*"

"100?!" Diego hissed, "but what about—"

"Worry about yourself," she wagged her finger at him as his body sucked up the colours, "we will be fine. You *need* it."

"I don't need shi—yooowch!"

She dug her sharp nails into his skin. "A proud idiot is a dead idiot! He's too fast, you *need* it. And besides, it'll ease our nerves, knowing you can counter him if he comes for us."

Diego looked on into the distance some more.

"Fine," he said. "Come here," he grabbed them, "we're hauling ass right back. Enough time wasted."

Before they could say a word, he sprinted right back to the battlefield. Kashmere's *Quick Yellow* splattered behind him as he picked up speed, spilling onto the dark roads.

CHAPTER NINE

They're here! Clara's eyes darted over the open road in front of her apartment. The wide boulevard had 4 lanes of traffic that were currently not in use as it was too late into the night for a car to pass by.

On both sides, the boulevard was flanked by tall, dark, grey buildings without much personality. The only colour that washed over them was that of Gilbert's red light flaring now and then.

Where...where are the rest? Why is it only Gilbert?

"Hey, Butterfly!" Lighting roared from somewhere down the road. "Where the hell did those 3 go? Did you see?"

"How the hell should I know? I'm a little busy right now."

"Yeah, yeah...I—"

Clara saw it at the same time as Lightning. Diego's large figure blitzed onto the scene, a trail of yellow left behind with each move. He darted down the boulevard, reaching the BMWs and putting Cole and Kashmere down.

"Guys!" Clara shouted.

"Cla—*dios mío*—" Diego shuddered, and, without even thinking, he unbuttoned his shirt and flung it at her, "wrap this around yourself, woman. I am weak of heart!"

The sky lit up at once.

"That's me, guys," Diego excused himself. "You two, fill her in and get going, alright?"

"Fill me—" Diego sprinted away, cutting her off as he clashed with the speedy Lightning, holding him off for the moment.

"Clara!" Kashmere jumped and embraced her, "thank God you're alright."

"Where's Sykes?" Cole asked.

"One of those three cars, I suspect," she started wrapping Diego's shirt around her waist.

"We did see them trying to take off in those," Kashmere nodded. "Let's check."

They dispersed, looking into the cars.

"Here," Cole called from the BMW in the middle. "There's something like a cocoon in the back, is that him?"

The two women gathered round, peering in.

"Has to," Clara nodded, "oh, stop," she caught Cole's hand just in time, "look," she pointed at the orange butterflies clinging to the doors. "The orange ones explode. He detonated one inside my apartment."

"Oh...shit," Kashmere muttered. "We would've been toast."

"My bad..."

"Doesn't matter now. We need to get him away from here and we need to do it now. Then, when we're safe, we can think of getting him out of that thing. Try to find a way in, I'll—"

She pointed her SMG at the passenger side window, yet just as she was about to shoot, Cole simply pulled the door open.

"It's unlocked," he said, "who wants to drive?"

The boulevard flashed red, again and again. At the upper floors of nearby buildings, lights came on as people looked out to see what was taking place.

The lower floors had already been ravished, the windows blasted through, the walls crumbling, dust filling the broken apartments.

Gilbert's whole focus was on Butterfly. Even as the car alarms blared up and down the streets from all the shockwaves. Even as the sky lit up and Diego clashed with the other, *his* sole focus was Butterfly.

His index finger curled, a red laser beam erupting out of it. Butterfly swallowed the attack, like all the others, regenerating just as quickly. As he curled his finger once more, he saw one of the BMWs taking off, yet as he was about to aim towards it, he noticed that Clara was behind the wheel, Kashmere sitting in Cole's lap in the front.

"Where the hell—"

An orange butterfly fluttered quickly towards him, just as the sky lit up and a surge of lightning hurled itself at the car. Diego followed the lightning, hurtling into it and dragging it away from the BMW, letting the wheels skid and carry the three away to safety.

Gilbert felt the flutter of wings nearby.

"Shit," he groaned. It was too close to shoot.

He dashed backwards as the butterfly burst. A large ball of fire scorched the air, the flames quickly dispersing.

As Gilbert staggered to a standstill, he sniffed at the air.

"Don't tell me you burned my fucking eyebrows off," he grimaced, fingering his face to see. "Fuck's sake," he sighed. I'm going to look like a clown because of you."

"Going to?" Butterfly turned his head, thoughtfully pinching his mask chin.

"It's all subjective, isn't it?" Gilbert stuck his hand in his pocket, taking out a cigarette. He popped it in his mouth, flicking his finger towards the tip and lit it with his laser beam, inhaling deeply.

"Are you seriously taking a cigarette break?"

Gilbert shrugged. "It's not a break—"

"Then?"

"—it's called stoking the fire."

Gilbert curled two fingers into his thumb. He flicked like before.

The boulevard filled with a yellow glow. The windows on much higher floors burst, sending shards flying down into the street. In their fall, they reflected the yellow light and took on the appearance of golden snowflakes, rushing towards the ground.

The air took on a charred scent as nothing resisted the burn of Gilbert's laser. Some odd trees were sprinkled here and there on the pavements, but their leaves were all burnt now just from indirect heat.

The attack itself *whizzed* and *banged* right into Butterfly's pelvis, disintegrating it and detaching his torso from them.

Instantly cauterised from the heat, his guts did not spill out as the torso fell onto the floor. Gilbert aimed his fingers again, this time at the fallen torso, and shot.

Yet just as it happened, Butterfly threw out his tie. His mask, for the first time, turned yellow. This new light rushed down the tie and unleashed a new set of butterflies, butterflies which clumped together and absorbed Gilbert's attack.

Not a single trace of his laser made it past.

He shot again...and again...and again...until he noticed the butterflies growing larger.

"Huh," he shifted the cigarette from one side of his mouth to the other, "that's intere—"

The butterflies peeled their bodies away as a great amount of yellow light emanated off them. It all shot back towards Gilbert, returning his firepower.

The whole boulevard erupted with a blinding light. The massive beam shot all the way down—so far, it went, that its end could not be traced with the naked eye.

Diego slammed Lightning into the ground floor of a building as they clashed. They broke through the concrete wall and found themselves within a—now ravaged—book store.

"Are you even human?" Lighting spat, getting to his feet.

"What kinda question is that, *cabrón*? We're both Crafters."

"What did you call me?"

"Not repeating myself," Diego clapped his hands together.

Chains crinkled as his Crafter Log appeared. He quickly clutched it and slammed it face down onto the floor. Cement formed into a mound, rising from below, twisting the floorboards, splintering them. Pages and books and bits of broken shelves shot up in the air as the giant block hurled itself at Lightning.

The hairs on Diego's arms started to frizz up with static. Lightning bolts shot and crashed against the block, spearing through it, shattering it.

Diego kept materialising them, firing away, hurling them forward. Each new block shattered with more difficulty, particles of cement shooting in all directions, piercing the walls and shattering into adjacent rooms.

His hands were kept on the floor as he kept on hardening the cement mixture.

After a little while, a smile appeared on Diego's face.

Gotcha!

He stretched his arms out and slammed his palms flat on the ground. Cement bubbled up around him as he then threw his arms forward. Large walls rose on both sides, shooting forward, flanking Lightning.

"What the—"

Diego arched them towards one another, seeking to slam them shut. As they rose, they tore through the ceiling. Parts caved in. Debris fell from the upper floor, crashing against the arches, yet they closed in quickly enough as the tunnel engulfed the two men.

"What the fuck?!"

"It's the pain-train from here on out, cabrón!" Diego howled.

"Alright, then, asshole, bring it!"

With a smile on his face, Diego clapped his hands together. In the darkness, cement spikes shot from the walls, seeking to pierce right through Lightning.

"Aha!" the tunnel lit up from his lightning. The brief flashes allowed Diego to see as Lightning twisted his body, evading his attacks.

"Stop this shit!" Lightning's voice echoed. He threw his fists after the spears, trying to shatter them, but they retreated too quickly.

He punched nothing but air.

"Aaaaarggh!"

"What's up, not quick enough?" Diego cackled. "Come on, cabrón, you were the fast one, no?"

"I'll show you *fast*."

Lightning started rubbing his feet quickly against the floor, building up energy. It crackled around his legs as Diego continued his onslaught, trying to catch and impale him.

Lightning advanced. His speed increased tremendously. Diego could not keep up with him. The spears fell inwards from all directions, yet Lightning weaved right through them.

In the blink of an eye, he closed the distance. He slammed himself into Diego's large body. An explosion of lightning rippled through the tunnel with a loud *hiss* as Diego was thrown back against his own concrete wall.

The wall withstood it, but then Lightning came again, ramming his knee against Diego's skull, slamming him into the wall again.

"Pain train, bitch?!" Lightning cackled, grabbing Diego's throat, lifting him, "for *who?!*"

The mask lit up with lightning as he drew his head back. He hurled himself right against Diego's face, crushing him with the toughness of his mask.

A massive burst of lightning coated Diego's body as he was shot through the end of his tunnel. He got propelled back into the boulevard, rolling violently onto the road. As he came to a stop, his body emanated fumes, a low hiss spitting out from his muscles.

Light no longer flashed up and down the street. It was a dark, still place. Even the moon itself shied away from casting its glow upon the world.

This guy...he's too dangerous, Diego rolled onto his back. He felt Kashmere's colours waning as he looked up at the distant building floors. He saw faces still courageous enough to look down from balconies. They were so small. So far away...so...helpless. *Goddamit.*

"Seems like you're all talk, huh?" Lightning slowly stepped back onto the boulevard. His body was coated in yellow electricity. It cracked with a great anger, whistling with energy. "What will it be? How do you want to die?"

"Who said anything about dying?" Diego got himself on his knees, breathing heavily. He looked on and saw as electric strands spread through the street. They shot up buildings, cracking the very walls.

Everything was crumbling.

I need to contain him, no matter what. He's caused enough damage already. Puta, look at me, trying to be protective. So fucking uncool.

"I mentioned it, actually," Lighting put up his hand

"Ah..." Diego sighed.

His Log appeared once more. His hands slammed onto the ground and another tunnel formed. Lightning looked up, hands akimbo.

"You're really trying for that, *again*?"

"What if I am, *punk*?"

"Alright, now *punk's* too far..."

Lightning reached out his arms. His palm filled with electricity as massive balls of lightning formed in them. He then twisted his palms, the two balls almost touching as he stretched his arms away from one another.

"*BOOM!*" he shouted.

A wave of electricity burst forth towards Diego. He hunkered down, bringing cement up from the ground and wrapping it around him, forming a bunker for himself. The lightning passed by him, but Diego wasn't as fast to move afterwards.

Lightning coated his fists in electricity and dashed forward, punching a clean hole through the concrete. As his knuckles met with Diego's chest, they tore a hole through it too.

Yet he was not propelled backwards.

"What the hell?" Lightning groaned, feeling a harsh clutch around his forearm. "Let go, asshole!"

"Nah," Diego spat blood, his chest torn to shreds. He held both hands tightly around his arm. The cement crumbled from around him. His face was pale. "Got you..."

Cement spilled out of Diego's fingers. It etched itself into Lightning's skin, sinking deep like a heavy tattoo.

"What the fuck! Let go, man! Let go!"

Come on, Diego gritted his teeth, *faster...it's not fast enough...*

He felt it spread through Lightning's body, rushing up his arms and into his shoulders, coursing its way towards his heart.

"LET!" Lighting's whole body burst with electricity. A net of electrified veins streaked Diego's whole body as the current caught him. "GO!"

The explosion cracked the road beneath him as Diego's whole body darkened, thumping onto the floor.

*Shit...*he thought, *it's cold as hell...*

Butterfly's torso left a trail of blood behind itself as he dragged himself towards his legs. They were still standing upright.

"This was supposed to be easy," he groaned, finding the cuffs of his suit pants. "We're going to be in deep shit. Fuck. Fuck..."

He clutched at his own ankles, pushing his legs over.

"Shit," he grimaced as they fell the other way. He dragged himself around, spun on his back, and then pushed his upper body against the maimed waistline.

His mask lit up with pink light as butterflies spread over his whole body, stitching him back together.

Further off, Gilbert got to his feet. He looked down at his left side, not uttering a word.

His whole arm was missing. The reflected blast took it clean off. Luckily, the heat of the laser cauterised the wound instantly, so he didn't bled.

Aches like a motherfucker, though.

His hairs were charred and the scent of coal could not be removed from his nostrils, no matter how hard he tried.

He looked on in the distance and saw a tunnel of cement splitting the boulevard.

"He's still holding up, then," he muttered, just realising that his lips were devoid of a cigarette.

He took one out and slotted it in place. A brief flick of the finger lit it up with a sparse, red laser.

"Alright," he inhaled, watching the pink butterflies disappear as his opponent got to his feet. "Still kicking, I see," he stuck out his hand

"I don't like you one bit, cigarette man," Butterfly shook his head. "I'm sick and tired of this shit."

"Ah well," Gilbert shrugged, flicking two fingers against his thumb.

Yellow beam burst forth, yet by the time he flicked his fingers, the *absorbing* yellow butterflies burst forth, swallowing the beam and instantly firing it back.

Gilbert threw himself to the ground and rolled, evading the beam. As he got to his knees, Butterfly already dashed forward, extending his tie as his mask grew orange.

"Mhmm..." Gilbert groaned, extending his hand.

One finger flicked. A red beam shot, exploding an orange butterfly before it could get near.

He flicked again—another burst. And again...and again...

The explosions propelled hot air towards him, forcing him to squint his eyes. His suit coat fluttered in the wake of all the chaos as he tried to get himself to his feet.

It was then that the burst of electricity filled the street.

"Woah..." Butterfly turned, "what was—"

"Idiot," Gilbert fired. The yellow beam hit his upper torso. Putting a hole right through his chest. Quickly, he fired another, right towards one arm, taking it off, and then—"

"LIGHTNING!" Butterfly roared, "HELP A BROTHER OUT!"

As Gilbert flicked for his other arm, electricity coated the streets. A flash of light came and picked Butterfly up, setting him aside, out of the beam.

"Where's Diego?" Gilbert spat, firing straight away at Lightning.

"Wooop," he burst with lightning again, moving Butterfly aside as he dodged. Another shot, and another. All missing. "Easy, man."

"I'll go easy when I—"

Butterfly was left there as a bolt of electricity rushed Gilbert. As soon as it got close to Gilbert, it turned itself into the shape of a man.

"Hey there," Lightning said, "need this finger?" and he suddenly latched onto Gilbert's thumb. Before he could react, Lightning twisted and pulled, breaking the bone and yanking with such speed that the whole thumb broke away from his hand.

"Huh," Gilbert smiled, "so this is how it feels."

"That's all?"

"*What*, do you want me to scream, you asshole?"

"What did you call me?" Lightning cocked back his fist.

"*Ass-hole*," he enunciated. Gilbert brought three of his fingers and pushed them into his palm.

"You pu—"

"Lights out," Gilbert flicked all three fingers. White light started to clump up in his palm, turning into a ball. Gilbert squeezed harder and the whole thing exploded like a bomb.

The city grew silent, the blast casting long, thick shadows over the entire world, engulfing it in darkness more than light.

The explosion left a tremendous crater into the ground in its wake. Two of the adjacent blocks had chunks taken out of their bodies, as if some beast had bit into them.

They no longer stood straight, instead, toppling towards one another, their tops crashing as everything crumbled down into the boulevard. Glass shattered and rock crumbled. Invisible metals groaned as they bent, unable to support the weight of all the toppled buildings.

The air was scorched and hard to breathe.

A bolt of lightning bounced against the ground a couple of times, skidding around the crater as he came to a stop.

"Fuuuuuck," Lighting croaked, his body gone up to his ribs.

"You're in a right mess, eh?" Butterfly stood over him, looking down, hands in his pockets. "What's Boss gonna think?"

"Just...shut up...man," Lightning struggled to speak. "Some help?"

"I'll get in trouble if I don't," Butterfly shrugged. "I like all the skin I still have."

"Then get to it."

"Yeah, yeah."

He crouched down, his mask glowing pink as the butterflies spread over Lightning's body, starting to fix him up.

"You think Boss—"

"You stop about that. Boss is not here," Butterfly looked up, "and my car is gone. I don't know if he took it and left. Now *that's* not dandy. What about our noodles?"

"We said we're not going for noodles anymore, remember?" Lightning sighed, "we were going to have Monica cook for us."

"Oh...yeah. Some food will be really good right now. Say," Butterfly looked down, "how many more meals do you think we got in us—lifetime."

"What?"

"What we do," he shrugged. "Ain't no easy thing, right? It's dandy, sure, but I mean—just today I thought I was going to die with an empty stomach. I'd be depressed if that happened."

"You'd be dead, you mean," Lightning corrected, "no time to be depressed."

"Nah, I'd find a way. Ane empty stomach bums me out real good. You're going to get promoted, you know?"

"As if!" Lightning spat. "What's gotten into you?"

"You took care of that big old fella," he pointed back over his shoulder, "and you got Laserfuck to blow himself up, too. With boss gone...I'll be alone here in this universe."

"Are you brooding?" Lightning cackled.

"Can't a man be sad for losing his friends?"

"Alright, yeah, sure. But—" he coughed. "Can I heal in peace?"

Butterfly shrugged. Pink butterflies continuously materialised all around him, their wings fluttering as they went and sacrificed their bodies for the sake of Lightning's regrowth. He looked over his shoulder, startled.

"Anything wrong?"

Butterfly hesitated. "I don't know," he shrugged. "I thought I felt something."

"Must've been the wind."

"Hup, two, three, four! Hup, two, three, four! Hup, two, three, four! HALT!"

Dmitry Fyodorovich Brazarov marched towards an apartment block, coming to a stop in a perfectly calculated arm's length from one of its walls.

He reached his old hand outwards and pressed his palm against the wall.

"*Bunker*ification complete," he said. "ATTEEEEENTION!" he roared, turning on his feet, eyeing down another building, unmarked, "Hup, two three, four! Hup, two, three, four! Hup two, three four!" he shouted as he made his way towards it.

His legs were completely straight and his arms were at his side, stiff, as he stomped his feet on the ground.

""Hup, two, three, four! Hup, two, three, four! Hup, two, three, four! HALT!"

Once more he stopped an arm's length away from the wall of the building, placing his palm against it.

"*Bunker*ification complete!" he shouted, "AT-TTEEEEEEEEEENTION!" and then turned and went on his way again towards another building.

Sykes slowly awoke from his slumber. A car engine revved with a great deal of anger all around him.

He opened his eyes. He was stretched out in the backseat.

"Clara?" he called, startling her.

"Sykes?!" she turned around. "Sykes, holy shit!"

"Where are we going?"

"You have some explanation to do, mister!"

"Hello to you, too, Kashmere," he sat up. "God dammit," he scowled.

"What's the matter?" Cole turned. "God, Kashmere, can you scooch into the back seat, please?"

"What are you implying?"

"That my legs are *numb*," he groaned.

"Whatever," she rolled her eyes, "coming through," and made her way in the back, right next to Sykes. "So I guess we got out of that guy's range, or what?"

"Seems so," Clara nodded, peering through the rear-view mirror at Sykes. "What's wrong with your hand?""

"Shit," Kashmere hissed, "it looks broken. Aah, get it away..." Kashmere drew further from him, unable to look.

"She's just squeamish," Cole turned in his seat. "Let me see."

With a great deal of strain, Sykes brought his hand up for Cole to see.

"Why?" Cole looked into his eyes, "do you know?"

"So I can't Craft," he said.

"You can Craft?!" Clara hissed, almost swerving off the road.

"Keep us straight!" Kashmere shouted from the back, "and head straight for HQ. We've got Sykes, right? We should head back."

"She's right," Cole agreed, materialising a pill in his hand.

"Is that for me?"

"Mhmm..."

"Mr. St. Jane," Clara cleared her throat, "so that in my apartment...you *were* crafting? It wasn't just my imagination."

Sykes shook his head. "I can't control it much. It seems it only wants to come out when I'm in danger."

"Infantile Crafting," Cole smiled. "Well, it's something, I guess."

"So..." Sykes hissed, "can I get that pill? This hurts like a bitch."

Cole hesitated.

"What's the matter?"

"I don't think it's a good idea," he shook his head.

"*What* isn't?" Kashmere mustered the courage to turn. "He can *fight*, right? Until we get to HQ, we only have *his* protection. We *need* his hand."

"I know, I know," Cole gritted his teeth, "but...I'm sorry, Sykes, but, those guys, they were *strong*. You...you're just discovering your powers, you can't match them."

"I can try."

Cole squeezed his forearm, making him wince. His eyes watered as he stared somewhere distant.

"I've been here before, Sykes," he told him, "I can't—"

"Stop it, Cole," Clara muttered, but her words lacked power.

"Hey, Cole," Sykes called, "come on, look at me."

"What?"

"It's *my* choice, alright? Whether you heal me or not, I *will* fight, *somehow*. I know you want to protect me, but you can't take away my own choice. It's my life to do with as I please. If I decide to put myself between you three and the enemy, that's my *choice* to make, not yours."

"But...*why*? We barely even met, you—"

Sykes whimpered, hesitating for a moment. He looked aside, then down, keeping his eyes to the car floor.

"It's not as heroic as it seems, but the reasoning is *my* reasoning. It's my son. If they're after me, they might be after him. You understand?"

"I..."

"Whatever it is, I gotta make it to HQ. I got to find Vulcan and make sure he's alright, even if it costs me my life."

"Then how—" Kashmere asked.

"You guys will do it, right?" he turned to them, his eyes red and wet, "if I die...you...you will check in...like you do with Grigory and—"

Cole suddenly clamped his hand around Sykes' nape, dragging him in. Their foreheads slammed together.

"Listen to me," Cole muttered. His breath was heavy, his eyes just as wet. "You're *not* dying, alright?"

"Cole, I've made up—"

"I know, dammit! I know! I won't stop you, god-knows I want to, but I know I can't. I couldn't before with *him*, I can't now with you. But I *can* help."

The four of them were silent. Clara kept her barefoot on the gas as she checked in on them through the rearview mirror, watching as Sykes' eyes were locked onto Cole's.

"I have a pill," Cole whispered. "Not this one," he threw the one in his hand away. It fizzled out before it hit anything. "But another. Much stronger."

"Sweet..."

"Much more dangerous, too."

"I don't care."

"*I* do," Cole dug his fingers into his nape, pulling him closer. "And *you* should, too. If not, at least you need to know what it does to you. I won't let you take it otherwise."

"Cole," Kashmere whispered, "what are you giving him?"

"I've been working on something since Grigory died," his voice shook. "It's unstable and it takes a toll on the body. It's *not* complete, God, it's not even approved. No one knows about it but I. But listen, Sykes, if push comes to shove, it's yours!"

"Fine, man, fine, but *what* does it do?"

"You have *two* minutes," he said, "from the moment you take it. In those *two* minutes, your body's regeneration rate is inhuman. Think a lizard regrowing its limbs, but to *all* of you.

The downsides," he added, "is that a significant portion of your life-span is reduced."

"Significant?" Sykes asked, "nothing precise?"

"No," Cole pursed his lips. "I didn't have enough time to gather specifics. But your body is on overdrive, *constantly*, those 2 minutes. The toll...it's immense. But...if it's needed..."

"I get it," Sykes nodded. "Give it here."

Cole kept their foreheads pressed together. Kashmere's hands clutched the car door handle, her nails anxiously chipping at the plastic.

Sykes put out his hand. Cole gripped it, as if shaking it, and instantly, Sykes felt a small tablet appear in his palm.

"Tha—"

Clara suddenly slammed the brakes. Cole was thrown against the dash. Kashmere banged her head against the seat in front of her.

Sykes nearly shot out of the windscreen.

"What the hell!?" Kashmere roared from the back, "what was that for?"

"Look," Clara clutched the wheel with both hands as she looked ahead.

As the other three recovered, they followed her gaze.

The cover of a man-hole popped right in front of them. That sight alone would've been quite formidable if it was any normal man-hole, but it wasn't.

The cover was a circular part of the night-sky, it popped and slammed into the ground, revealing a hole into it, leading to an *other* side.

A man in a white suit crawled out of that man-hole, clutching with his leather-gloved hands at the edges of the sky as he stuck his stone-masked head out to look at the four of them.

"That's him!" Sykes erupted. "He was the one I saw at Icarus!"

They all turned to him, the information new.

Sykes threw himself right out of the car.

"Mr. St. Jane, wait!" Clara shouted.

"SYKES!" Cole roared, "THE PILL!"

"I know!"

"Remember, *two* minutes!"

"Hold on just a minute," Clara turned in her seat, "don't let him go just like that. Kash," she looked, "give him *something*."

Kashmere shook her head. "My *Quick Yellow* and *Strong Green* are 100% on Diego, look," she said, bringing her hands forward.

The two colours bubbled up in her palms. Her face froze.

"Kash..." Clara muttered, "what...what does that..."

Kashmere looked up. Her head shook slowly, side to side, as her eyes began to fill with tears.

Cole looked from one to the other.

"Dammit!" he slammed his fists into the dashboard. "I thought...I thought he didn't need—*FUCK! FUCK! FUCK!*"

"Done with the tantrums, you four?" the masked man called from down the street.

He was standing right in the centre of a T-junction. The roads were completely empty.

"Kashmere," Sykes stuck his head back in the car. "I...I don't want to sound dismissive, but could I—"

"What?" she looked up at him, startled. "Oh..." she looked at her hands, at the colour. "Right...*Quick Yellow, Strong Green—100%*" She whispered with uncertainty.

His body surged with colour. He stepped forward, yet just then, Clara rolled down her window, catching his arm.

He turned and looked at her. Her eyes were large, dark pools. He dove right into them, swimming around in her despair.

"I'll be fine," he said. "I promise."

"Please..."

"Cole. How fast does this thing kick in?" He looked down at the pill.

"Instnatly."

"Alright," he popped it in his mouth. "I'll see what I can do."

Without another word, he pulled away from the car. Clara's arm fell limply as she stared at his back, growing ever-distant.

"Kind of me to let you have your little moment, don't you think?" the masked man asked. Red semaphore lights flared out over the whole intersection, coating him in an ominous light. "I'm Noodle, by the way. I don't appreciate you speaking over my entrance."

"We've met before, Noodle," Sykes stretched out his fingers, his hand no longer broken. "Haven't we?"

"Yeah. By chance, really."

"Both times?"

Noodle shrugged.

"It's not chance now, is it?" Sykes asked.

"What do you think?" Noodle turned his head, quizzically.

The semaphore lights turned green.

Sykes burst forth with a rapid sprint. The speed he was going at was something he had to get accustomed to. In a few steps, he covered the distance between them and at first wasn't prepared to reach him so quickly.

"We're not staying for a chat, then?" Noodle asked. He brought his arms backwards. The two tube-like barrels in his palms swung right back, wanting to slam into Sykes' chest.

Sykes evaded, a deathly gust of odourless air shooting out. He threw a quick punch for the ribs, but Noodle slammed his elbow down and blocked it. He turned his palms for Sykes again; another burst.

Sykes dashed backwards, putting some distance between them. It was then that he noticed the empty space suddenly liquifying as the bursts of air spread out. *Space* itself frayed and separated into multiple threads, ones which Noodle reached his hands for to grab.

He held them like ropes, pulling them back.

The night sky and the bits of a building and pavement and fence that were there, caught in the blast, suddenly yanked away, leaving behind them an *absence* of space as Noddle whipped the ropes through the air.

They cracked like thunder, air bursting out of them. Sykes had the speed to dash away.

What the hell is that? And what will happen to me if I get touched? Do I turn, too?

He suddenly clawed his right hand and with a yellow trail in his wake, he appeared behind Noodle.

The anger within him made it so there was no trouble materialising the dark ball within his palm.

He punched forward. Yet just as he was about to slam the black-hole into Noodle's back, the man twisted his head 180 degrees and tutted.

"*Tsk, tsk, tsk,*" he sighed, "you think it's that easy?"

He jumped up in the air, dragging his legs after himself just as Sykes punched forward, hitting nothing.

The ropes dragged, cracking up and down the intersection, their echoes spreading over the whole city as they hurtled at Sykes.

They came too fast. He couldn't evade.

He simply held his hand outward, increasing the output of his Crafting capability as the ball of darkness grew wider inside of his palm—wide enough to welcome all of the slinging ropes and to swallow them out of existence.

"Huh," Noodle landed a little ways off. The lights turned amber, briefly. A momentary pause cast itself over them. "So you're telling me you're *not* just a coincidence?"

Sykes didn't understand the question, yet neither did he want to.

"How interesting," Noodle drew his arms back. His palms pumped air, dragging more ropes into his grip. This time, as he pulled them back, he clutched at them separately. A part for his left hand, one for his right, this way, he had two frayed whips to be working with.

He started slamming them against the ground. The whole road was starting to curve and fluctuate as if a great body of water suddenly appeared beneath it. Sykes steadied his footing, looking intently at the man before him as he quickly whipped the noodles towards him.

His right and left hand swung at once. The whips came at him from both sides. Sykes brought his hand towards his right, planning on sucking up all of that rope once more, whilst trying to benefit from his speed in order to dodge the one coming from the left.

Shit, he hissed, realising his mistake.

The two batches of noodles came at him with the same speed. There was no time to do what he planned. They were going to crush him in between.

He was frozen. The right noodle-rope disappeared into thin-air, sucked up by his black-hole, as the left slammed into his legs, ripping the ground from beneath his feet as his body began to stretch and wind as if he, too, was made out of the same substance as Noddle's whips.

Sykes thudded against the floor, groaning, using his hands to drag himself further away from Noodle.

"Sykes!" Clara shouted, stepping out of the car. "Shit, we should be doing something! We're just watching!"

"We can't do anything, Clara," Cole held her as she tried to run forward. "He's too strong for us."

"And he's not for Sykes?"

Cole said nothing for a moment.

"Is he *not* for Sykes?" she gasped as she repeated herself.

"We've put all our faith in him for now," Cole told her, matter-of-factly. "He has my drug and he has Kashmere's paint."

"For 2 minutes!" Clara threw her hands up in the air. "What do we do *after?*"

"The director sent the Upper Six," Cole looked down into the ground, his voice but a whisper. "Once they come, all will be good."

"Right...*once.*"

"You have to put *faith* in him, Clara," Cole's eyes shot up. "Look at me," he put his hands up, "you see? I'm shaking. I *know*. I'm here with you—but...it's just how things are. We *must* wait."

Kashmere was still in the car. The side of her head rested against the window as her body shook with sobs.

"Aaaaagh!" Sykes suddenly roared. Clara and Cole turned to look at him.

They saw him on the floor, slamming his own ball of darkness against his own, undulating eggs. He gritted his teeth as blood splattered in all directions, his legs whisked out of existence.

A metallic scent burst into his nose, as if the blood was coming straight from there.

"What the hell are you doing?" Noodle stopped. "This has got me scratching my head," he said, "have you given up that quickly?"

"Nuh—" Sykes panted. His whole face was red with the horrible pain he had just endured. "Gaaaah!" he continued to grunt and huff and puff as right away, stumps started to appear out from the bottom of his torso, everything growing back into place. "Christ...aaaggh..."

He had not expected the growing of limbs to hurt, yet it was pain he had to endure. There was no other way.

Once regenerated, he got up to his feet.

"Well," Arthur groaned, "that's a sight."

Sykes looked down. His legs regenerated, sure, yet his pants did not. It mattered very little, in the heat of things. He quickly sped towards Noodle.

The masked man slammed his palms onto the ground.

Like before, the ground bent and fluctuated, yet with much more intensity. It was difficult for Sykes to run over constantly shifting ground and at times he tripped and almost fell onto his face.

The annoyance made him halt, trying to look for an alternative. He looked at his palm and remembered his dream. He remembered when he was reaching his hand towards his own son and pulled him close.

He took a deep breath and did the same just now. He held his hand forward, aiming it at Noodle. The ball began to swirl in his palm—and then, it happened.

He was getting closer to Noodle. At first, slowly, yet then, as he realised it was actually working, he intensified the amount of power and the space between them *shrunk*.

In reality—he made it disappear altogether. The black hole within his palm sucked up the time and space itself that stood between them, bringing Sykes closer much too quickly.

"Shi—" Noodle gasped, pumping more air into the ground. He managed to fluctuate it just enough that the denivelation between the two of them shifted their positions, and, instead of Sykes' hand slamming straight down from his head into the rest of his body, he had caught just the side of him, swallowing his ribs and half of his torso before he managed to get away.

Sykes looked up, expecting to see blood splattered onto the road and the mutterings and whimperings of a dying man. He saw instead circuitry sparking and oil spilling onto the road.

"What the—" Sykes narrowed his eyes, "*what* are you?"

"Me?" Noodle asked. "What do you mean? I am just like you, aren't I? I am out here, dismembered, fighting for my life."

"But you—"

"Listen to me," he said. "Is a human the flesh, the blood, the bone and the marrow? Or is a human the *mind*?"

"I don't—"

"I am just like you. I am blessed with sapience. I am aware of myself and those around me. Just because my blood is darkened oil and my flesh is metal, that does not make me less human."

"Sykes," Clara shouted, "don't listen to him! Get away from there!"

Sykes didn't understand at first, yet then, a masked woman stepped into his field of vision.

He recognised her.

"Shit," he gasped, "you too?"

"We are partners, I'll have you know," she said, her voice filtered. "How did he get you in such a state, Noodle?"

"Cybress..."

"Don't you make excuses. If you do, I won't build you back up."

"Just you wait until you see his ability," Noodle spat, "you'll have a fit."

"Just tell me. I am *not* patient."

"How about I show you?" Sykes asked, ready to dash forward. Yet as he took his first step, he realised that his speed was back to normal.

"What the—?"

Cybress chuckled. That chuckle grew into a hearty laughter that echoed down the streets.

"Take a look, you poor thing," she pointed past him, "oh please do."

A little hesitant, he turned around. Cole, Kashmere, and Clara were on the ground, right by the car.

Three masked figures, all wearing the same mask as Noodle stood over them, their palms aimed at their bodies.

"You—" he gritted his teeth, "leave them alone!"

"I will," she nodded, "if you come with us, that is."

"Why would I do that?"

"I've just been told you've got an interesting power. You shall be of use to us. And besides," she raised a finger to her stone lips, pretending to think, "you don't want *more* of your colleagues to die, do you?"

Sykes no longer listened to her. He stretched his arm out towards the stoned figure standing over his three friends.

The ball in his palm grew to an incredible size and in the blink of an eye—not only had he swallowed up the space standing between him and the stone figures, but he had pierced through them and swallowed them completely.

No trace of them was left.

"You guys alright?" he asked, looking at them. Kashmere was completely out.

"Yes, Sykes, yes," Cole muttered, getting to her side, checking her pulse. "She's fine," he assured him. "*We* are fine. But you'll have to do without her paints. Can you manage?"

"I'll manage."

"Good," he nodded, "then hurry, you don't have much left."

As he turned, Clara sat with her knees pressed to her chest, wrapping her arms around them, watching him throw his life away.

You're weak, she scolded herself, *you can't do anything. You're always in the heat of things and can't do a damn thing as everyone gives their all...*

Some of the lights still flickered to green over the broken T-Junction.

"He really is quite strong, huh?" Cybress murmured. "Now I don't blame you for getting yourself in this state that you are in, Noodle. Well," she sighed, "I suppose he won't go quietly into the night, will he?"

She clicked her fingers. Noodle started to grow his parts back, getting to his feet as even his suit made use of metallic fibres to sew itself together.

As soon as he was standing on his feet, he looked brand new.

"Where did we leave off?" Noodle asked.

"You go and get him," she sighed, "not *kill*, just *get him*. Understand?"

"Yes, yes, I mean—"

"I don't want to hear it. We got no time. We need to go."

"Are we in a rush somewhere?" he asked.

"Yes," she nodded, "which is why I gave you some improvements. Now make use of them and get him."

Sykes heavily debated what to do. He knew that he couldn't just leave his friends there but at the same time he couldn't properly fight whilst hovering over them.

I have no choice, he said to himself, *I have to get in there and fight and not give them a chance to take them.*

He clawed at the air and swallowed up the space in between them in an instant. At first, he was nearing closer to them, but then, Noodle stretched one arm sideways, sucking up the space into noodles, whilst with the other hand he pointed right at Sykes.

Through one hand, he sucked in the noodles from his surroundings, passing them through his body and onto the second arm which outstretched in front of him.

Everything shot out of it and towards Sykes.

"If you're going to devour space, then devour it," Noodle shouted, "I can feed you all night."

Frustrated, Sykes increased the output of his power, until he felt that it reached its limit. Noodle's limit, though, didn't seem to be anywhere in sight. He continued to take strips of space out of the surroundings, black strands of nothingness left behind in the place of a lamp post, or a car, or the side of an entire building.

Even parts of the sky itself disappeared, as if someone had peeled off a plaster and revealed the true nothingness underneath.

For a moment, Sykes wondered what would happen to all of that empty space as soon as the battle was over.

Will it return? Will it forever remain a strip of nothingness that no one could touch otherwise they'd disappear just the same?

Passing thoughts—thoughts which occupied his mind as his heart was racing, realising slowly that he was losing the battle of attrition.

He was getting pushed back, his arm giving in. Unable to accept defeat, he dropped to his knees. He threw his hand aside and sucked in the space, moving himself towards the right.

From this new angle, he moved the hand right back, hoping to get an advantage as he sucked the space between them once more, hurling himself at them.

It happened so quickly that he thought he got them. Yet just as his black-hole was about to swallow them up, he hit a wall.

"What?" he groaned, pushing harder.

The wall was invisible at first, yet shortly, sparks exploded in all directions.

"As I thought," Cybress chuckled, "not quite potent enough to erase my cyber-wall. Good to know."

A sudden pain burst over Sykes' arm.

"It seems he wanted to come to me first, Noodle," she said, "perhaps I upgraded you for no reason."

Sykes looked at the source of the pain. The tip of her black pumps pushed right through his elbow. Blood gushed out of the wound as her leg remained perfectly extended.

Come on, he gritted his teeth, *come on come on come on. Has it been two minutes already? Fuuuuck!*

"Are you dozing off?" she asked. Her hand was around his throat, clutching it. "You need to look at me."

As Sykes looked up, he caught sight of the golden mark on her wrist. From up close now, it resembled a tail.

He looked up into Cybress' eye sockets.

His eyes moved to the stone-mask eye sockets.

"Ci—" he started. "Cia—"

She slapped him across the face.

"It's not good for you to know that," she said, bringing her hand towards his head. A whirring noise escaped out of her fingers as she pierced his skull "There. Now it's gone. Come on, Noodle," she tutted, "store him inside of you and let us get out of here."

"What about the other three?"

Cybress took a look at them. "We have no use for them."

"Let me dispose of them."

"No," she said, "don't."

"Huh?"

"There's no point. They are too weak, they pose no threat to us and our organisation. Not only that, but they cannot provide them with new intel. What these people know about us won't change if we let them live."

"But—"

"I *won't* have them killed."

Noodle grumbled something and nodded. He placed his palm against Sykes' ribs and—

From somewhere distant, shouting ensued. It was a singular voice, steadily approaching

"HUP, TWO, THREE, FOUR! HUP, TWO, THREE, FOUR! HUP, TWO, THREE, FOUR! HUP, TWO, THREE, FOUR! HUP, TWO, TRHEE, FOUR—HALT! — AIM! — FIRE!"

A thick bullet whizzed through the air, piercing through the cyber-wall, Cybress' elbow, Noodle's stone mask all at once, escaping out the other side.

Sykes dropped onto the ground as a shutting-down noise whirred out of Noodle.

Blood and bone splattered out of Cybress' elbow but she made no sound.

She caught onto Noodle and sent currents through him, repairing his head.

"What the hell was that?" he asked, "who was…"

"RELOAD!" the old man's voice echoed through the dark streets, "AIM! — FIRE!"

Another bullet came.

It whizzed for Cybress' head, yet before it hit her, Noodle pushed her out of the way. It grazed the side of his face, removing part of the stone mask and most of his jaw and cheek and all of his ear.

"Twerp," the old man shouted. Sykes turned towards him. He was wearing a full black suit. He was bald and wrinkly and his eyes were as vast as the night sky. "Get out of there. I bought you enough time."

Sykes gulped, looked around, got to his feet and dashed away.

"Go next to your friends," the old man shouted, "you will be safe there."

Safe from what? he wondered, running away.

"Sykes!" Clara jumped in his arms, embracing him. She was shaking all over. "You're fine!"

"Who is that guy?"

"He's—"

"I am DMITRI FYODOROVICH BRAZAROV!" the old man roared his name, bursting with pride. "You make sure to remember the name well so when you reach hell, you can tell them who sent you!"

"He's one of the Upper Six," Cole said, "let me see your elbow. Damn...it's bad. I can't give you another pill. Not so soon after the previous one. You'll have to endure for now."

"I'll be fine," Sykes spoke as Clara still clung to him. "I'm fine, Clara. It's all good."

"AIM!" Dmitry shouted, "FIRE!"

They all turned to look at him. There were no weapons anywhere in his clutch yet somehow he had fired two bullets faster than the eye could see.

He had his hands folded behind his back. He didn't aim a single thing, yet from the centre of his face, a bullet burst and flew towards Noodle.

Noodle was ready for it. He pumped air out of his large palms and undulated everything, turning even the fast bullet into nothing but a harmless noodle which he sucked up into his body—and then, miraculously, lashed it right back.

"Watch out!" Sykes shouted, but the old man simply inclined his head towards the side a few inches, the bullet whizzing right by his ear.

He betrayed no emotion.

"You are not the weakest scum I've encountered. Your *woman*, what is she for? Is she the one wearing the pants? I do not like that," he said, "that is not the traditional way. Back in Russia we—"

"Oh would you shut up?" Noodle started to turn the whole road into noodles. The man walked steadily, holding his hands clenched together behind his back.

"Very well. I will shut up."

He kept to his promise. For the remainder of the battle, he hadn't opened his mouth once.

Sykes watched him walk as bullets started firing rapidly out from before him. They were all kinds; large and small calibre alike and everything in between. They cut through the air with barely any sound and Noodle was stuck trying to suck them, blocking them from reaching his body and Cybress' alike.

Dmitri turned on his feet. He faced his four colleagues, not caring for anything that happened behind him.

The bullets kept on firing, yet now from the back of his head, keeping Noodle occupied.

"Where are you looking, old man?"

Noodle sucked up all the bullets and then fired them back out. They were elongated but they had the same firing power as he managed to keep their velocity.

With a shudder, Sykes gripped Clara's head and tucked her close to him as he stretched over her. Cole did the same for the unconscious Kashmere.

"Don't worry. You and your friends are in no danger," Dimitri spoke to him softly. "You defended your comrades valiantly. I respect you, young man. Rest easy, right now, the biggest danger to you is me."

"Wh-what?"

Bullets kept flying out of him and back his way. Those which had an adequate trajectory of hitting Dmitri or to come too close to Sykes and the others, Dimitri shot specific bullets to meet them on the way, splattering them, the shrapnel exploding away from those he sought to protect.

It wasn't long before Dmitri stood tall right in front of Sykes. He kneeled down and spoke over the artillery fire.

He had to shout. "Look up for me," he told Sykes.

He was blocking Noodle's view of Sykes, so as Sykes turned his head to turn upwards, his face dropping, only Dmitri could see it.

"Wh-what the hell is that?"

"It's a bomb," Dmitri said matter-of-factly.

It stood there, floating in the air, waiting to be dropped.

"Wait, no, please," he tried to reason, "you'll kill—you'll kill so many people, so—"

"I have years of experience in warfare, *twerp*," Dmitri spat. "I won't kill anybody. You think I've run this late out of my own free will? The streets will burn, so will the trees. But the people and their homes will live. It's only you four and those two behind me which are not protected, you see?"

"So you plan to drop it?"

"Of course."

"Wh-when?" Sykes' voice faltered as he kept on looking up at the bomb.

"It's falling as we speak," Dmitri smiled. He took one hand out from behind his back and placed it onto the ground. It shifted and started swallowing Sykes and the others up. "Don't worry. You'll be safe and back up here in no time."

Sykes tried to say something in return, but he was submerged completely into the ground.

"*Bunker*ification complete," Dmitri said.

"Hey, old man—"

"ARTHUR!" Cybress shouted, "ABOVE US!"

Noodle turned his head and saw the giant bomb approaching. "SHIIIIIIT!" he threw himself at Cybress. He dropped his mask, gaping his mouth wide as the bomb exploded before hitting the ground.

Everything grew quiet.

Dmitri stood up, facing the blast, not covering himself.

"How beautiful," he said, his eyes flashing with the blinding brightness as the ball of fire started to swallow the city.

CHAPTER TEN

A man-hole appeared in mid-air within a vast room made out of stone walls. Arthur fell out of that hole, dragging Cybress after him.

The two were panting wildly.

"That is one old fool," Arthur gasped, "what the hell was he thinking? He must've eradicated the entire town with that. And for what—just to get rid of us?"

"Just be glad I warned you," she sat up, and then stood. She brushed some dust off herself and looked around. "Where did you bring us?"

"It's better you don't know," Arthur muttered. "Much safer this way."

Cybress stood up, pacing the room. Her footsteps made no sound. Somewhere, a stream of water trickled in the dark.

She found herself stepping on moss. Soft, a little mushy.

"It smells..."

"Like a forest," Arthur said, "I hope."

"Close enough," she admitted. "Was this all your doing?"

As Arthur got up, he made his way towards one of the four walls, flipping a switch. A low light slowly emanated from the ceiling, beaming down like a weak sun.

Some small trees were tucked in a corner, together with a pond. A swing hung low from one of the boughs. Between two trunks, a hammock stretched out.

"What is all this, Arthur?" she looked at him briefly, but then returned her eyes to the retreat.

"My place," he said. "But—leave that. What about the city just now, the bomb?"

"What about it?"

"Cianna…" he stepped forward, wrapping his arms around her from the back. "It's *your* city. Your friends, family—what about them?"

"They'll be fine," she purred, running her hands over his, squeezing herself against his body. "Where's the bed?"

"What would I need a bed for? I don't sleep."

"After all this time, *sleep* is still the only thing you think about when it comes to a bed, huh?" she sighed, pulling away. "So unserious."

"You can't be the one calling me unserious right now. It doesn't add up."

"It adds up just nicely."

"Just tell me," he begged, "Did you *see* what that guy—Sykes—was using?"

Cianna froze.

"Did you see or did you not?"

"Of course I saw," she said.

"*And*, you have nothing to say to that? I mean, he was right under your nose and—"

"Listen to me, Arthur," she hissed, "*you* are the one made to fight. I made *you* to fight my battles. You are the one that failed to secure him. Are you even *aware* of how good it would've been for me if we captured him?"

"For us, you mean."

"For us, yes, whatever," she waved the comment away.

"I am aware, yes," he nodded. "I am *also* aware of the fact that we fucked up. It's not going to be good."

"Yeah," she paced around, looking at the ceiling, scanning the room from wall to wall. "Are you sure this place is safe? They cannot see us here?"

"They cannot see us nor hear us nor detect our pings. It is as if we vanished..."

"As if we were dead?"

"Sure," he nodded, "but without a corpse."

"I see," she pushed away from the wall. "So I suppose I really can't get you to go out there and get some proper beds for us, right?"

"No."

"Alright," she nodded, walking right back to him.

"What do we do now?" he asked.

"Now?" she smiled, taking off her mask, "now we enjoy ourselves, and after, we *think* and plan our next move."

He looked into her lustful eyes as she pressed her mouth against his metal face.

Ah, he thought just then, *that's what she wanted a bed for.*

Gilbert found himself standing at the entrance of a bar. It was lit with a low-orange light. The length of the bar seemed a little immense.

Flanking his path towards the bar-counter were an innumerable amount of tables, all with silent people seated at them. Some looked at him, some looked into their laps. None spoke.

It was total silence.

He looked towards the end of the path, at the bar-counter. Instead of stools, there was one hammock strapped to two poles flanking the bar. A beautiful Asian lady stood behind said counter, wiping a kerchief on the inside of a pint glass.

"Isn't your throat a little dry?" she called.

"How did you know?"

"I can tell a thirsting man when I see one," she smiled.

"That can mean *two* things."

"I know."

He stepped forward slowly. His footsteps made no sound. It was as if he *stepped* on nothing.

"Can I smoke in here?"

"Of course."

He reached his right hand in his pocket. He took a cigarette out, rolling it between his thumb and forefinger before he placed it in his mouth.

He brought his nail into his thumb and was about to flick.

"Nuh-uh," the woman called. "No Crafting allowed."

"That's a policy?" he sounded surprised. "Since when?"

"Since I said so. Come here," she put the pint and kerchief down and reached beneath the counter. She held a silver zippo lighter with a cloud pattern etched into it. "You want to smoke or not?"

"So no Crafting, huh?"

"None," she nodded.

"Alright."

He got up close to the bar. As he walked, he could sense the people's eyes following him, stopping to cling onto his back as soon as he reached the bar. Once he did, leaned over the hammock and looked into her eyes as she flicked the lighter, lighting his cigarette.

He inhaled, took the cigarette out of his mouth, looked at it, placed it back.

"Who's this hammock for?"

"For you," she said, returning to her business of cleaning the pint, "for customers," she corrected herself.

Gilbert groaned as he got himself into it. Instead of stretching out his legs inside of the hammock, he stuck them out and crossed them onto the counter.

"Hey, that's—"

"Don't worry about it. You won't get in trouble with your boss, right?"

"I mean…"

"Tell me, lady. What's your name?"

"Yumeno," she said.

"Yumeno," he repeated. "Nice name. Japanese?"

"Yes."

"Well," he shifted a little in his hammock, suddenly sitting up, his legs still stretched and crossed on the counter. "Come a little closer, Yumeno, won't you? I want to ask you something."

She looked at him oddly yet did as he requested.

"Tell me what you think of this smoke," he said, slowly blowing out all that he inhaled into her face.

She took it all, unflinching, and then smiled.

"It's smoke."

"Ah," he smiled in return, placing the cigarette back in his mouth as he leaned into the hammock, crossing one arm behind his head. "You smoke, Yumeno?"

"No."

"Well, I do," he said, "a lot, actually. I smoke so much that I can tell one bad cigarette from another. This," he pinched it in between his fingers and took it out of his mouth, scrutinising it, "this is not a cigarette at all. The smoke is not the right temperature," he said, "it has no taste, and, when it goes down my throat, it doesn't scratch it at all."

"You might've smoked a little *too* much."

"You're very polite," he nodded, "and for that, I am grateful." He placed the cigarette back in his mouth, shaking his head. "Tell me," he looked aside, "is Diego dead, too?"

Yumeno's smile faltered for a moment.

"It's okay," he sighed. "Don't make this awkward, alright? There's no need. I am aware. I was aware since I got here, look," he pushed his fingers into his thumb and aimed at her, "*poof*," he flicked, yet nothing came out. "No Crafting allowed," he chuckled. "It's a little too obvious."

"I see," she muttered.

"So? Did he kick the bucket or not?"

"Not quite yet, no," she shook her head.

"That's good," he sighed. "Big fucking oaf. I don't know how he does it. What about the people?"

"Sorry?"

"The people here at the bar. Civilians I killed, right, with my last attack?"

Yumeno said nothing.

"A little cruel, don't you think?" he chuckled. "Having them be here."

"Not at all."

"No?"

"No," Yumeno stood firm. "Ignorance might be bliss for the human mind. Yet in the realm of the dead, it is a matter of *soul*, not one of *mind* . A soul cannot be ignorant. A soul must look its burdens in the eyes if it wishes to ever attain peace."

Gilbert nodded slowly.

"*All* of them?" his voice faltered as he lifted his head, looking down the path at the filled tables.

"*All.*"

"I see."

He laid there a moment, staring blankly into nothingness.

"Say, Yumeno, how much time have I got here?"

"A good while," she said.

"Good," he groaned, getting up and out of the hammock. He started walking around until he found himself an empty chair, somewhere thrown aside. He picked it up and carried it towards the first table in his path. "Bring us some beers, won't you?" he asked her, "and that lighter. I'll provide the cigarettes."

Yumeno smiled as she watched him place his elbows onto the table, throwing the packet of cigarettes in the centre as he took in all those people's faces.

"Oh," he suddenly said, "and an ashtray, won't you?"

"Coming right up!"

Yumeno's feet did not touch the ground. Instead, her pumps stepped upon little white clouds, forming before her.

She floated over the giant crater.

To her left were the two masked figures; the perpetrators. To her right was the dying man they called Diego.

Yumeno turned towards the left.

Two clouds engulfed the masked figures' faces. The two men were completely out, flat on the floor. One of them had his legs built only as far down as the knees, the rest was missing.

The other was intact.

She stepped towards them. At their side, she raised them up to her level with the help of her clouds.

"How crude," she pouted her lips, the clouds peeling back from their masked faces. The tops of their skulls were still coated in the clouds, which kept them asleep, in a constant dreaming state.

Yumeno's fingers pressed against their masks. In an instant, they snapped in two and fell towards the ground.

"Yuck," she sneered at the sight of their skin-peeled faces. "I much preferred you two with them on. It was a mistake to take them off," she sighed, letting the clouds roll back over their faces.

Yumeno then turned and walked towards Diego.

"Are you still alive?" she asked, crouching down, placing her hands on her knees as she looked at his wounds. "I told your friend Gilbert that you are. Was I mistaken?"

"H—how is he?"

"He's not with us anymore."

Diego said nothing.

"Tell me, where would you like to be right now?" she asked.

"I'd...I'd like to see Gilbert."

She sighed, taking a better look at his wounds.

"I can do that for you."

"Just for a bit," he grunted, trying to move, "I'd like—just to tell him—"

Yumeno nodded. A little cloud formed a halo over Diego's head. The pained look on his face slowly washed away, turning into a smile.

"I'll be quick," he said. "I'll tell him to wait for me wherever it is he's going."

"Sure," Yumeno stood. "You do that."

Out of her pant-suit pocket she took out a cellphone. She contacted the one *true* number between the hundreds of dupes saved in it.

"Clear on my side, Director," she said, her eyes still looking at Diego's smiling face. "I'm afraid not, Director. I was too late. I see. Yes. Are you sure? Very well. I'll stay here until they arrive. Good-bye."

Weeks later, a procession crawled through town. Everyone at Icarus—with the exception of three people—were present, following the two hearses carrying Diego's and Gilbert's bodies.

The roads had been blocked. No personnel from the media was allowed to get anywhere near—although some have tried.

Nobody spoke but in a whisper.

Clara, Cole and Kashmere were at the very front of the procession, right behind the two hearses driving slowly side by side. Clara and Kashmere sobbed

Cole held it together, somehow.

Behind them, led by Metnick Deep, the director, were the others which were closest to the two killed in action. Lexi Cormick, his personal assistant, also walked at his side.

Santiago, Diego's best friend, held his head high. His eyes were red and his dark jaw protruded from how hard he was gritting his teeth. Stacy Carri's plump, pale lips quivered as she held back from crying. Simone Trii and Khalid Engles walked hand in hand, trying to comfort one another.

They walked the two all throughout town, the procession holding 3 whole hours.

Nobody complained about the walk; the two deserved it and much more.

At the end of those 3 hours, the hearses led the way towards Icarus' private cemetery. It was a large, open field. The tombstones were flat on the ground and were carved to resemble a feather. From a crow's point of view, each of the tombstones connected, the feathers uniting to create two beautiful wings.

Once the road finished, they took down the coffins from the hearses and carried them by hand towards Diego's and Gilbert's burial spots.

They were side by side.

The official air seemed to dissipate as soon as the people found themselves around the graves. The silence got pierced by Clara's and Kashmere's sobs and she led the way for others to join in. Metnick Deep was dressed all in black, missing his signature apparel. It was no place to take away from the sacrifice of two heroes.

He stared directly into the two graves as the coffins were lowered at the same time. As dirt started getting shovelled in, it sounded as if someone was banging a hammer against his skull.

It throbbed and throbbed and throbbed until he could take it no longer, but he stood his ground.

He almost lost his footing, but Santiago caught his elbow as if nothing had happened at all.

The two men exchanged glances and nods in total silence. There was no need to speak. Their red eyes said enough words.

Once the dirt piled up and flattened out, the stone feathers got turned over and dropped on top, digging into the ground and locking themselves in.

Later, when people started to leave for their homes in order to live through the sorrow in their own ways, only a few remained by the two graves.

Metnick Deep stood with his hands in his pockets, staring up into the sky.

The rest were all there, wrapped around like a crescent moon.

"Terry didn't come," Clara whimpered. "He *didn't* come," she looked away, trying to hold onto some sense. Cole reached for her, pulling Clara close to his chest. The front of his suit soaked in her tears. "And Sykes...where...where is Sykes?"

"Cianna...too..." Kashmere whispered.

"Those two men would've come, Clara," Metnick Deep spoke, "if I allowed them to. If you are to get angry at anyone, get angry at me, not at them."

They all turned their attention towards the director.

"I would rather not discuss *business* here, though," he said, feeling everyone's gazes on him. "As for Cianna..." he sighed, shaking his head, "I don't know. I haven't seen her since. No one's found her. But let's not worry about that now. This is a place for mourning, is it not? We should respect these two as they pass on to wherever it is that they are going."

"Straight to hell for the both of them," Santiago muttered.

The Director cracked a smile.

"Yeah," he sighed, "maybe. Considering what some of us people are able to do with our bodies, I wouldn't think God is much too happy with us."

"If we are to go by that logic God might have forsaken humanity a long time ago," Simone added in a quiet voice. "It's been a while since we've been defying nature."

"Has it now?" the Director asked, "I suppose," he sighed again. "But knowing that doesn't make any of this feel any better. We're all doomed, are we not?"

"Depends how you look at it, Director," Santiago said, "if most of humanity is getting sent to hell, considering how unruly we are, I'm sure by the time we get there it will be like we're back up here on Earth all over again."

"You say so?"

Santiago sighed. His cheeks sucked in as he started chewing on them. "I'm damn sure of it," he said. "With those two down there as well? Psshh..." he chuckled, "I can see them already setting up some bars. Or maybe they're going around looking for cigarettes."

"Maybe, yeah," the Director smiled. "Either way," he turned around and faced them all. "We failed, *again*," his voice was coarse. "We've been caught off-guard and we've lost two members of our family. It's..." he looked at the ground, digging the tip of his boot in the dirt. "It's unacceptable.

He let a moment pass. He looked up, took a deep breath, nodded, started again.

"I wouldn't blame any of you if you no longer feel it safe to work under the name of Icarus. The world is tumultuous enough as it is."

"Director—"

"Quiet, Santiago," he placated him with his hand, "I am not finished. I will not hold it against you if you decide to resign. *But*," he raised his finger, "I also have an alternative: a facility. It will house all employees, Crafters and Non-Crafters alike; *maximum* security at all times. Now," he tried for a smile, saw he couldn't make it land, and gave it up. "You aren't forced to reside there, but I *highly* recommend it. Even so," he sighed, sticking his hands back in his pockets, "if you still decide against it, I will make sure to have guards posted at your personal residences for protection."

"That's going too far, Director, don't you think?" Santiago blurted.

Director sniffled his nose. He stepped towards Santiago, craning his neck to look at him as he kept his hands in his pockets.

"Don't be daft," he shook his head, slowly, "alright? Not now."

With those words, he excused himself, leaving them to mourn.

EPILOGUE

Sykes was alone in a small room that resembled a prison cell. All four walls were white, as was everything else.

He was the only splash of colour in that room.

The way things were arranged, it gave off the impression that he was floating around somewhere and not actually with his back pressed against the wall, sitting on a bed.

It must be the light, he thought, *or maybe the way the material bounces it away.*

There was no temperature in the room. The concept of hot or cold did not exist. He even lifted his hand towards his mouth and tried to blow some air onto it, but he felt nothing.

It was as if everything was suspended.

He got up to his feet. As he brushed against the bedsheets, there was no noise. He opened his mouth, blurting out something at random.

"......"

His vocal chords made no sound. His lips, neither, as he tried popping them together.

Am I dead? He wondered, starting to walk down one way to see just how big the room was.

As he placed one foot in front of the other, he started to think.

His mind raced back to the last thing he remembered.

The bomb.

*'Bunker*ification complete,' the words echoed.

The darkness came right after. No sound followed. He was certain that the bomb had dropped.

He remembered the old man's smile. A shudder crept up his spine.

He was still walking ahead. He had walked around 200 or so metres and he still didn't hit the end of the room.

Sykes continued walking some more.

He didn't remember anything that had happened right after that.

His mind suddenly filled with worry for his friends. A cold sweat spread over his whole back as he tried to tell himself that all was well.

He was unravelling slowly. His mind was losing itself inside of the white room.

He traced the steps of memory even further back. He started thinking about his son. A silly thought crossed his mind, making him wonder whether the masked figures were after him as well.

His heart raced.

He started running forward, trying his hardest to reach the end of the room, hoping to find a wall that he could break through.

He ran and ran and still reached nothing. He tried to go faster and faster, desperate, his lungs aching with strain, his muscles just as well. He reached out his right hand and then an idea came to his mind.

He focused his attention to it.

Wait, he thought just then, *what...what happened? Wasn't this snapped from the elbow down?*

He brushed that aside quickly. What mattered was getting out of the room.

He stretched out his arm, trying to summon the black orb in order to suck up all the space between him and the end of the wall.

Nothing happened.

Come on, he thought, straining himself, yet no matter how hard he tried nothing came out.

It was just then that the white wall slid away, forming a door.

On the other side of that door stood Terry Finster. Giant, dark, scrawny.

"We meet again, Muffin Man."

"Terry!" Sykes tensed up. "Terry where's my son?!" he howled, "How long have I been here for? Is he okay—is Montana—"

"Your family is fine, Sykes. Icarus has them under their protection."

"I-Icarus? So this—this is—"

"Your questions will be answered," Terry cleared his throat. He leaned back and pressed something on the other side of the wall.

The lights dimmed out in the room and something that wasn't there before came over him.

That was silence.

As soon as he heard it, he stopped and Terry stepped into the room, the door sliding shut behind him.

Terry only paced halfway down the room before he stopped, looking at Sykes.

"Calm down," Terry tried to assure him. "We're not holding your family against you. They're being watched."

"Watched?"

"In the protecting sense," Terry clarified, raising a placating hand, "not the *keepin an eye on them* sense. You understand?"

"Why?"

"As I said—all will be answered. Come on, let's sit down."

As Sykes turned, he noticed that he hadn't even moved from the side of the bed. Everything was still as white as before but now with the lights dimmed down, he could see the contours of objects. He could clearly see the bed and a table with two chairs right opposite it.

As he looked down, he could also see the floor which was one large and white treadmill-band.

"This is a confinement area," he said. "It is not the only one, but it *is* the only one that confines you. That make sense?" Terry waited for him to respond. "Who thinks of this?" he continued, seeing that Sykes had nothing to say. That's what you must be wondering, right? The answer is, *we do*. Please," he waved to the chair opposite him, "sit down. We must talk."

"You said my family was safe."

"That I did," Terry nodded. "And I am no liar, Sykes."

"What about my friends, then?"

"Your colleagues, you mean?"

"S-sure," Sykes nodded, finally sitting down. The tension slowly dissipated from his body—yet not all.

Terry towered over him even as the two sat down, one white table across.

"Which of them are you concerned with?"

"Clara, Kashmere, Cole, Diego, Gilbert and Cianna Deep."

"Diego and Gilbert were killed in action."

"Wha—"

Terry raised a hand to stop him from speaking.

"Cianna Deep is gone missing and the rest," he sighed, "are currently attending the funeral procession. It is a pity that we weren't permitted to go, but I understand and in due time, so will you."

"Understand what?"

"Everything, I hope," Terry smiled. "Your mind is clouded and a clouded mind cannot see the path beset before its feet. We must clear away the clouds."

"O-okay."

"That is what we are doing here," he said.

"S-sure, but—"

"I will come out and say it, Sykes. There is concern at Icarus that a spy is among us," he said. "As of right now, the signs point to you."

"To me?" he sounded shocked, "but I—"

"We are not getting to the defence part yet," Terry stopped him. "Right now, I am putting all that there is to be put onto this table right here," he waved his hands over it, "and once the cards are down for the both of us, we can start discussing."

"Clearing the clouds..."

"Exactly," Terry nodded. "I am glad you picked up on it. "Now, as I was saying. We have reason to believe that you might be a spy. These reasons are as follows: 1. You have applied to join Icarus several times over the course of several months." he said. "Each and every time," he then continued, "you have failed to meet the minimum criteria and were rejected. Either way, you tried again and again. Some might deem that strength of character, others, might consider it a plot against Icarus."

*Oh God...*Sykes shook his head, *this is exactly like that time with Gilbert...*

"2. All of a sudden, you stroll into Icarus and get examined once more. You break all of our scanners, yet somehow you are only deemed a Muffin Man. Your power level is barely that of a C-Crafter. In addition, you claim to have had no epiphany, and, it was made clear to us that it was quite evident you in fact, didn't.

"3. We are quite certain that you withheld crucial information about these masked figures which attacked you and Clara that night weeks ago. We also hold the belief that all—and if not all, at least the deaths of Diego and Gilbert—could have been avoided.

"4. Although you are considered to barely pass into the ranks of a C-Crafter, on the night of the attacks, you held your ground against what we identified as a mixture of B-Crafters and M-Crafters.

"Now," he sighed, "as you can see, that is quite a lot. I understand if it takes some time for you to register what—"

"Before we continue," Sykes' words rushed out of him. "I need to know one thing."

"Ask away," Terry smiled, "and if I can answer, I will."

"Will my confession affect the way Icarus will view my family?"

Terry pursed his lips a moment and then sucked them in. "It depends."

"Like *shit* it does," Sykes slammed the table with his fists. "My family has *nothing* to do with any of this. They wanted *nothing* to do with this. It's all *me*, dammit! All *me—my* fault!"

Terry smiled. "Do they *know* anything?"

"Not a *damn* thing."

Terry laced his fingers on the desk, tapping his thumbs together as his smile slowly faded into a neutral, yet searching face.

"So?" Sykes breathed heavily.

"So what?"

"Are they still safe? My family, are they—"

"Not as safe as you'd hope," Terry said.

"Is that...is that my fault, too?"

Terry nodded. Sykes' eyes searched for something both men in that room knew he wasn't going to find. His body deflated slowly.

"How...how can we change that?"

"We are working on it, Sykes," Terry assured him. "As of the moment of your capture at the hands of Dmitri Fyodorovich Brazarov; 99% of the people who knew you have no recollection of you having ever existed. The exceptions, currently, are your family and the closest to you at Icarus, including myself, the director, and his assistants. By the end of this interview, only those here at Icarus would be aware of who you are, Mr. St. Jane."

"No, please, I—"

Terry lifted another placating hand. Silence fell over their bodies and Terry made use of it to stare a moment into Sykes' rheumy eyes.

"From this moment on, Sykes, you can consider yourself as a man without existence," he said, his voice final, like a nail closing a coffin shut.

9 798218 576783